THE
HEROIC BARON

Other books by Nikki Poppen:

The Dowager's Wager

THE
HEROIC BARON

•

Nikki Poppen

AVALON BOOKS
NEW YORK

Published by Thomas Bouregy & Co., Inc.
160 Madison Avenue, New York, NY 10016

Library of Congress Cataloging-in-Publication Data

Poppen, Nikki, 1967–
The heroic baron / Nikki Poppen.
p. cm.
ISBN 0-8034-9807-1 (acid-free paper) 1. Nobility—Fiction.
I. Title.
PS3616.O657H47 2006
813'.6—dc22
2006024267

PRINTED IN THE UNITED STATES OF AMERICA
ON ACID-FREE PAPER
BY HADDON CRAFTSMEN, BLOOMSBURG, PENNSYLVANIA

For Rowan, who is seven and thinks Percy Blakeney and Robin Hood are the greatest heroes ever. Ro, you are a true classic. May you always love to read. Books are fabulous adventures. The hero in this story, Alain, is for you. He swims, he thinks, and he is a responsible man who looks out for the people he loves—just like you.

For Great Auntie Frances in Kansas who still walks to the library twice a week to stock up on romances and has never stopped believing in the power of love.

Chapter One

Fate had made Alain Hartsfield, the Baron Wickham for all of five days, her whipping boy. That dreadful muse had conspired with the mud-rutted roads and overworked axel of the carriage carrying his parents and fiancée, Alicia, home from London. Two miles from The Refuge, the strained axel broke, sending the carriage plummeting over the sharp embankment and its occupants to their deaths.

Now, all the king's horses and all the king's men couldn't put Alain Hartsfield's life back together again—an awful truth brought home to him in the stillness pervading the empty foyer. After five days of funereal obligations, he was finally and utterly alone. The quiet was eerie in the wake of the last departing guest, his sister Isabella and her husband Anacreon St. John the Marquis of Westbrooke.

His two friends from childhood, Chatham Somerset and Giles Moncrief, had offered to stay on but Alain

1

had declined the offer. He had to face facts sooner or later. He could not continue to put it off. Along with settling a haunting tragedy squarely on his broad shoulders, Fate also managed to endow him with a large burden of guilt. *He should have been there.*

Alain strode down the hall to the room that served as a library. He hadn't tried facing his failure with a strong glass of smuggled brandy yet. Perhaps that would work. He poured amber liquid from the cut-crystal decanter on the library sideboard into a tumbler and folded his long form into a worn, comfortable leather chair. He let the guilt come; he should have gone to London in his father's place as he usually did. He should have ridden out to meet them as he'd planned and not let the rain deter him. He should have ridden faster when word had come of the accident. The doctor who'd fortuitously been traveling the same road said Alicia had lived an hour or so after they'd pulled her from the wreckage. She had called for him. He had missed her by mere minutes.

If he'd been with them he would have noticed the axel before it was too late. If he had ridden out to meet them, he could have cried a warning in time to slow the coach. If he'd ridden faster, ignoring the danger to himself and his horse on those same muddy roads, he could have reached Alicia. If he'd been there, he could have saved her. Should haves and could haves tumbled in a misbegotten litany of grief through his mind until he fell into an awkward doze, the brandy at his elbow untouched.

Light streamed through the library window, causing Alain to groan and shield his eyes. Deuce take it all, it was bright. Some numbskull had drawn back the curtains. He opened his eyes to a squint and moaned when he realized where he was. *He* was the numbskull who had not bothered to shut the drapes. Last night it had been rainy and dark. There'd been no need to shut the drapes, and he certainly hadn't been planning on falling asleep in such a clumsy position. He shifted in the chair, grunting. No, he'd better rephrase that, such a *painful* position. His back ached and his neck had at least two cricks in it. Prior to this morning, he believed a person could only have one crick at a time in certain body parts. Last night proved him wrong. Alain glanced at the glass of brandy on the little table beside the chair. He was glad he hadn't drunk himself into oblivion. Waking up this morning was bad enough without a headache to contend with as well.

Alain stood and stretched his long body, reaching over his head with his arms. Besides, oblivion was only temporary. He still had to face the realities of his life. The servants at The Refuge would look to him for leadership. His grand vision to build a seaside resort in Hythe for vacationing middle-class families would falter without his direction. Whether he liked it or not, whether they should or not, people were counting on him. He'd failed three people in his life. He would not fail the others.

His valet, Cranston, scratched on the library door. "Come." Futilely, Alain straightened his rumpled clothing, knowing the meticulous Cranston would have an apoplexy upon sight.

To his credit, Cranston refrained from scolding, much to Alain's eternal gratitude. The loyal but stiff-necked valet merely cocked an examining eyebrow at his charge—Alain knew Cranston would always look at him thusly. Cranston styled himself as an artist, not as an employee. "My lord, I have laid out fresh clothes and your shaving things in your room. I will have your *dishabille* resolved in no time." He snapped his fingers to emphasize his point.

"Thank you, Cranston. When we're finished, please tell Harker I will take breakfast in the estate office. Send word to Daniel Mullins that I want to visit the project site after I eat. We have decisions to make regarding the 'grand vision' if we want to stay on schedule." It felt good to give orders. It imbued the day with an ordinary quality, as if his life hadn't been disrupted by tragedy. He felt almost normal. Perhaps, if he could carry on with business as usual, he wouldn't have to feel at all.

"Alain! I didn't expect to see you out today!"

Alain turned in his saddle to greet Daniel Mullins, friend and the architectural brains behind his vision. "We have deadlines to meet. People are counting on us to go ahead with the project." And he needed to stay busy so he wouldn't start hurting again. The "grand vision" was a soothing balm. The outlines of the buildings were already visible from his post up on the cliffs overlooking Hythe. Wooden pickets and white string marked the layout of his dreams. He had bricklayers and masons waiting to start laying the foundations of the three buildings.

"The weather is conspiring against us." Daniel edged his horse closer to Alain's big bay, cupping his hand to his mouth to be heard against the wind. "I'm not sure we'll meet any deadlines in the rain. We can't lay the brick foundations in mud."

Alain gave a frustrated shrugged. "The ground was too frozen in the winter to dig, and now the ground is too muddy."

Daniel reached over to clap Alain on the back. "Spring will be here soon enough. It's March. The bad weather won't last much longer. Besides, there's no hurry as long as the war with Napoleon is still on. War time isn't conducive to travel. Your backers won't be visiting until August after the Season lets out in London. By then, we'll have made an impressive amount of progress."

Alain nodded reluctantly. He was impatient. He wanted to move forward with the "grand vision." He wanted to see something tangible, to know that his efforts weren't in vain, that he was doing something useful with his life. The need to be useful was especially foremost in his mind this past week. Facing the mortality of others inevitably led to facing one's own mortality. He was going to die. *What would he leave behind? To what purpose was his existence?*

He had conceived of the idea two years ago, driven by a relentless case of ennui after his sister's wedding to Westbrooke. He'd watched his sister start her life as the marchioness of a wealthy peer shortly after his best friend, Tristan Moreland, departed to join the English Peninsular Campaign against Napoleon. The two people he was closest to had moved on from their childhood romps into adulthood, leaving him behind. To assuage his feelings of loneliness and abandonment, he'd paid a visit to Hythe, home of The Refuge, one of two Wickham family baronial estates.

The Hythe of his childhood was a quiet village. Historically, Hythe had been quiet for centuries since the thirteen hundreds. The war with Napoleon had upset the lazy balance in Hythe and the strangled war time economy had wrecked havoc with the people's abilities to provide for themselves honestly. As the heir to The Refuge, Alain felt responsible for their plight. They were his people. He'd known what he wanted to do so he called upon an old friend from Eton, Daniel Mullins, who was now a young, rising architect under the Prince's Regency. Then he'd gathered together backers who'd help financially sponsor the project.

"The wind is picking up," Daniel said beside him. "Let's ride down to the buildings. I want to check the stakes and make sure they hold."

Alain's spirits lifted as he dismounted a few minutes later after navigating the winding trail down to the village. It did him good to see the string outlines of his project. Even with this small amount of detail, he could fill his head with imaginings of Hythe as a bustling resort town. Not on par with Brighton, of course, a little further down the coast. It was not meant to compete with Brighton. His town was for middle-class families looking for an affordable vacation, an inexpensive escape from the oppressive heat of a London summer.

Satisfied that the stakes were secure against a storm blowing off the channel, Daniel suggested a mug of grog. "Everyone in town will be at The Sail and Oar except the most intrepid of ferrymen." Daniel stomped his feet and blew on his hands against the cold stirred up by the wind.

Alain laughed. "You try so hard to be a sailor, my friend. I am afraid you're a landlubber at heart."

"I am an architect after all." Daniel took the ribbing good-naturedly. "We can leave the horses up here at the livery and walk down."

The Sail and Oar was located on the currently quiet wharf. Gray whitecapped waves banged against the pilings, crafts bobbed defiantly at their strong moorings against the Channel's onslaught. Despite the cold outside, The Sail and Oar emanated the warmth of rich laughter and the camaraderie of men holed up for the duration. Indeed, many of these men had been holed up since the December storms made plying their sea-going trades impossible until spring brought calmer waters.

Upon seeing him, the men broke into cheers, forming a gauntlet of sorts to thump him on the back. Someone thrust a mug of ale in his hand. Someone else steered him to an empty seat at a bench amid them. Someone else, who he recognized as Matthew Hinton, the town blacksmith, raised a frothing mug in a toast. "To the baron!" The phrase chorused around him amid a cacophony of clanking tankards.

Alain dug in his purse for coins for a round of drinks. Matthew Hinton's beefy paw stopped him. "Your coppers are no good here today, are they men?" Hinton looked around at the crowded public room, eyeing everyone for approval. Everyone nodded in agreement. Alain took the kind gesture graciously. It was their way of mourning with him. In a small, warm way, the village mourning with him eased the foreboding sense of loss that had permeated his life over the last week. His family had been part of the community fabric for three generations. His loss was their loss. He was not alone in his grief. His quiet, stalwart father who worked diligently behind the scenes as well as his generous, more vivacious *émigré* mother would be missed by them all. His spirits improving, Alain raised his tankard for a second toast. "To Hythe and its good people!"

Suddenly the door whipped open bringing with it a rush of wind and spray and Matthew Hinton's eight-year-old son. He was soaked and panting. "Da, there's a boat! Ma sent me to tell you that it's breaking up. There are people on it! Da, you've got to help it."

Alain was on his feet next to Matthew. "Show us the boat, Tommy."

The scow was two hundred feet from shore and foundering. With the weather conditions as they were, it might as well have been a mile. Alain rapidly scanned the shore, his sharp eyes lighting on a sturdy row boat. He pointed to it, firing off orders. "Matthew, you and I will take the row boat out. Malcolm, take what men you need and get your boat underway." Alain scanned the gray waters one more time before jumping in the row boat with Matthew. "We've got to hurry; someone is already in the water!"

Alain's shirt was plastered against his skin by the time he and Matthew managed to maneuver their row boat close to the foundering little dinghy. With each stroke, the winds threatened to blow them off course, if not worse. Alain recognized his strength alone would not have gotten the row boat to its destination.

On board the sinking craft, a woman was shouting hysterically and pointing to the man in the water, while a small child clung to her wet skirts screaming. An older boy had the presence of mind to alternate his efforts between bailing water and attempting to reach the drowning man with a long pole. Both efforts were valiant but futile. The bailing bucket was no match for the wrath of the English Channel and the pole was too short, even if he could have kept the boat on course.

Acting quickly, Alain reached for the cordon of rope lying at his feet. He tossed it to the man in the water, who grabbed it desperately. Matthew steadied the boat with his massive blacksmith's strength while Alain tugged the rope, hand over hand. The man couldn't hold on. By Alain's estimation, he'd been in the water for ten minutes. It was miraculous the stormy waves hadn't already claimed him, but the cold was deadly. His hands were too frozen to grasp the rope. Alain sighted Malcolm's boat. It would reach them within minutes. "Get the woman and children into our boat and then transfer to Malcolm's," Alain instructed. "I'm going in after the man." With that, Alain secured himself to the boat with a makeshift harness and plunged into the icy waters.

At the best of times, the Channel was a cold place to swim. This time of year, it was positively frigid. Twenty glacial feet later, Alain reached the man's side. The man was barely conscious, the cold having sapped the last of his strength. At least that meant the man wouldn't fight him and drown his rescuer in the process. Alain gripped the man under the armpits and tugged on the rope, signaling Matthew to pull him back in.

Matthew pulled him aboard and Alain collapsed, shivering, alongside his rescued bundle in the bottom of the boat. Matthew threw a blanket around Alain.

"Take some rope and lash the boats together," Alain said between chattering teeth. "I won't be able to help you row back."

Matthew nodded. "I'll take care of it. Everyone is safe. Nothing left of the boat, though."

Alain squinted through the spray to where the injured boat had been. It was gone. It had sunk rapidly after his mad jump into the Channel. He put a hand on the chest of the man he'd rescued. The man's skin was chilly, his heartbeat slow but steady. Alain covered him with the spare blanket and began chafing his hands while Matthew arranged to get them safely to shore.

Back on land, Daniel waited anxiously to help unload the boats. Alain was glad to see his friend had arranged for blankets and a wagon to meet them. The family from the boat was in no shape to walk even the fifty feet to The Sail and Oar. Alain discovered he wasn't either. He would have fallen if Daniel hadn't waded to his aid after Matthew hauled the man ashore.

"Whatever possessed you to jump in the Channel? You could have drowned, strong swimmer or not." Daniel scolded, taking Alain's weight and dragging him to the wagon where he unceremoniously dumped him on the tailgate.

Alain took the dry blanket Daniel held out to him and huddled down into it, soaking up what small amount of warmth it provided. "I wonder, Daniel, whatever possesses a man to sail his family across the Channel in such weather."

"You are not going to stay and find out. We'll get you dry, and then you're going straight back to The Refuge. Cranston can look after you properly," Daniel ordered.

Alain protested. "I can't just leave them. These people are my responsibility." He looked down at his ruined boots. "Besides, Cranston will flay me for what I've done to his hard work on these Hessians."

Daniel sighed. "I'll be your eyes and ears. Let me get you settled, and I'll come back down to learn what I can."

Three hours later, Alain was significantly warmer but no less curious as he lounged by the blazing inferno Harker had insisted be built up in the library. Perhaps too hot, although it wasn't as hot as Cranston's temper after the valet had seen his boots. Of course, Alain knew Cranston's outrage over the boots was a cleverly disguised ruse to hide his chagrin over Alain's stunt in the Channel. Alain tossed off the lap throw draped across his legs. It made him feel like an invalid. Where was Daniel?

As if on cue, Harker entered the room and announced Daniel's arrival. "You're soaking wet!" Alain exclaimed over his friend's appearance. "Come by the fire and dry out. In a moment you'll be more sweaty than wet." He waited as long as he could before pestering Daniel for information.

"So, are you going to tell me what possesses a man to risk his family in such a manner?" Alain said when he could stand it no longer.

Daniel glanced at the mantel clock. "Five minutes. That's nearly a record for you. I was wondering how long you'd last."

"That's three hours and five minutes. Dash it, Daniel; I've been cooped up here for hours waiting on tenterhooks for you to return." Alain strode to the sideboard and poured his friend a drink. Coffee and sandwiches were on the way if he knew Harker, but brandy would be a good warmer in the interim. He handed it to his friend. "Teasing aside, thank you for going."

"Teasing aside, you are welcome." Daniel sipped from the glass before speaking again. "Here's what I know. I only got sense out of the boy. The mother was too distraught and the father, well, you know what shape he's in. Their name is Panchette. They're from France. They used to own a bakery, but circumstances being what they are in Paris, the family could no longer make a living. According to the boy, Gascon, they couldn't afford to make bread for themselves, let alone a neighborhood. Faced with starvation and eviction and nowhere to go, they decided to chance the waters and bet on a better life in England."

"What can they hope to do here?"

"Gascon says his parents hope to find jobs in service." Daniel shrugged, mimicking Alain's gesture of disbelief.

"In service? Hythe is hardly the place to do that, and they have no resources to afford a trip to London, which is their best chance at finding that kind of work. This venture of theirs seems poorly planned." Alain groused. He was silent, letting Harker settle the coffee service on the table near the fireplace.

"Shall I pour out, my lord?" Harker asked.

Alain cocked his head at Harker. "Does Cook need help in the kitchens? I've recently developed a penchant for fresh baked breads, tea cakes, and the like."

"I don't recall you having a sweet tooth before, my lord."

"There's always a first time, Harker. Tell Cook I'll be

sending a French baker to her within the week. Whatever he bakes and we don't eat, we'll send down to The Sail and Oar. The taverner will know how to put the extra loaves to good use." A stunned Harker left the room with a curt, "yes my lord."

Alain turned to see Daniel smiling over his coffee cup. "Stop grinning, Daniel. I've decided that if the baker and his wife work out, Hythe will be in need of a teahouse. I hear they are becoming popular in London. You can design it."

Daniel waved his coffee cup. "I'm not smiling at that. I am smiling at you. Just a moment ago you were cursing their flight as an irresponsibly managed adventure. Now, you're setting them up in business. You're generous to a fault. You've saved them just as you saved me."

Alain looked startled. He decided to play the sapskull. "Whatever do you mean?"

Daniel smiled indulgently. "I know what you did for me by giving me the commission for your 'grand vision.' You rescued me from ignominy. I was on the verge of quitting and looking for work as an assistant to a larger firm. You rescued me and my dream of being my own man."

Alain looked away, awkward with his friend's praise. "You were the best qualified man for the job. It didn't matter that you weren't famous." It hadn't mattered to him. He knew the depth of his school chum's abilities. Unfortunately, it had mattered to others of the nobility who could afford to build the mansions Daniel designed. Once Alain had taken up his case, commissions had flooded in. He returned to a more comfortable topic of conversation. "Did the boy say anything else?"

Daniel gave a wry grin. "I hesitate to tell you what else he said."

"Give over man, don't hold back." Alain cajoled.

"Well, it seems that the boy's cousins are still in Paris with no way to get out."

"Where there are cousins, there are aunts and uncles too, I presume?" Alain drummed his long fingers absently on the arm of his chair.

"Presumably."

"It bears thinking on." Alain rose from the chair and paced in front of the long window, looking outside into the falling darkness without really seeing it. His mind was already whirring.

Cautiously, Daniel asked, "What bears thinking on? I've seen that look in your eye plenty of times during our school days. It bodes no good."

"What look?" Alain protested, momentarily derailed from his conversation.

Daniel threw up his hands. "The one where your eyes start shooting green sparks and before I know it, you've dragged me into another madcap escapade like the time you insisted we had to rescue Tristan Moreland from the headmaster's office at Eton."

Alain shrugged, hiding a smile. "We got away with it. I don't know what you're complaining about. But that's not important now. What is important are the Panchettes."

"Truly, Alain, you can't be thinking to save them all."

"That's precisely what I'm thinking." Alain turned from the window, his face a mask of seriousness.

"Surely you're joking? I was only joking when I said it." Daniel looked beleaguered. He set down the coffee cup and reached for a fortifying swallow of brandy from the forgotten glass at his side.

"I assure you I am not joking. We should go get the aunt, the uncle, and the cousins."

Daniel sputtered, spraying brandy on the Aubusson carpet. "What about the resort?"

Alain's face lit with his enthusiasm, more enthusiasm than he'd felt since the tragedy. "Don't you see, they are the 'grand vision'! We're building a resort town for middle-class families, for people who aren't rich."

"What does a resort town have to do with poor bakers in Paris?" Daniel, literal and concrete to the last, puckered his brow.

Alain threw his arms wide, excitement radiating from him. "The new world, the world that will be in place after the wars are over is a world of equality; a world that will be accessible to people who are not nobility. We have an obligation to liberate people from oppression. It's already started. Ready-made clothes have made it possible for people to ape their betters. This is an exciting time, Daniel, the world is changing under our very feet. We will go to Paris and get the rest of their family. It will be our contribution to the new world order. What do you say?" Alain knelt down in front of his friend, looking expectantly at Daniel's face.

Slowly, comprehension dawned. Daniel nodded, repeating Alain's earlier words. "It bears thinking on."

"It certainly does!" For the first time in days, Alain was glad to be alive.

Chapter Two

"God bless you, my child." The old woman on the crudely constructed rope bed in the corner of the dim room reached up a gnarled hand in gratitude to cup Cecile's smooth cheek. "I hope you haven't given me more than can you afford to spare. There are so many others in need and there's your brother too, *n'est-ce pas*?"

Cecile tucked the frayed blankets about the woman. "We must all do what we can for one another in these times. Do not fret over me. I have work." Work that allowed her to pick over the spoils of the wealthy general's kitchen; work that allowed her to play her treasured violin every night in order to earn the largesse of the general and his friends while they sat around their groaning supper tables toasting the New Regime under Napoleon. For Cecile and others like her, the New Regime didn't look or act much differently than the old.

"I'll see you tomorrow. I'll bring medicine and a hot soup with a carrot." Cecile assured the old woman. She picked her basket up from the rickety table in the room's center and took a final look at the dingy lodgings, making a mental note of the woman's needs. Perhaps she might contrive to bring clean sheets. The maids in the general's household were doing the spring laundry that week. They might be willing to part with the old sheets set aside to be thrown away.

Cecile stepped outside into the brighter light of day, her thoughts on the list of errands she needed to run before going to the general's house that evening. The sunlight contrasted sharply with the dim interior of the old woman's room, and she collided with a brick wall before her eyes could adjust.

"Oof!" Cecile doubled over panting as the wind was knocked from her lungs. She dropped her basket and clutched her stomach. She'd been stupid not to concentrate on her surroundings. *What if I had fallen and broken an arm or even so much as sprained a finger or shoulder? What would happen to my brother if I couldn't play my violin?*

"*Pardonez-moi,* Mademoiselle, are you hurt?"

The brick wall spoke! Cecile looked up in surprise. The wall was a man—a tall, tawny-haired man with sharp green eyes the color of new moss that were studying her in interest. Cecile pulled herself up to her full height, just an inch under five and a half feet. She felt shorter than usual against the man's height. His intense scrutiny made her feel vulnerable.

"I am fine." Cecile replied brusquely, brushing at her

gray serge skirts. She gave the Apollo-like figure a cursory nod and attempted to step around him.

"*Attendez, attendez,* Mademoiselle," the man cried. "You've forgotten your basket. You must have dropped it when I so indelicately crashed into you." He moved to retrieve the basket from the narrow sidewalk, unintentionally providing Cecile with a view of his powerful body in motion. The stranger had exquisitely broad shoulders that strained the seams of his coat and long muscled legs that flexed divinely as he bent for the basket.

"May I ask you, Mademoiselle, if you know the residence of the Panchettes? I believe they are bakers, or at least they were once."

Cecile took the basket he handed her, assessing the stranger as he had no doubt assessed her moments ago. She had not seen him in the neighborhood before. She didn't dare trust him to be on an innocent mission. "*Je regrette,* Monsieur." Cecile shook her head and shrugged. "I do not know those people. If you will excuse me, I must be going." She made to step around him a second time, only to find herself blocked again.

A knowing smile formed on his lips, even as his mossy eyes grew jade hard at her response. His hand reached inside his coat for a wallet. He pulled out several franc bills. Cecile tried not to gape at the money. The sum would buy medicine for her brother and others, not to mention clothes and food and perhaps a doctor. He asked his question again. "Do you know where I can find the Panchettes?"

Cecile swallowed hard against the temptation. Someday the money would be gone, spent for good things, but her guilt would remain if anything happened to the

Panchettes. She would find another way to get the things she needed. She tilted her head at an angle, doing her best to look outraged. "I cannot be bought, Monsieur, not even for a lie."

The hardness melted from his eyes and his smile softened. "My apologies, take it for the truth." He reached for her hand and pressed the bills into it, curling her fingers around them. "I commend you for your principles."

Somewhere in the warren of tenements a whistle called out. The man's head jerked up, seeming to separate the sound from the usual whines and noises of the squalid neighborhood. "*Adieu,* Mademoiselle."

Cecile watched the stranger dart around the corner and disappear into an alleyway. His absence broke the spell that held her rooted to the sidewalk. Common sense returning, she thrust the enormous sum of bills deep into her skirt pocket. What had the man been thinking of to carry such an amount of money with him and to brandish it about so openly in the slums? He was lucky it had been in the quiet part of the afternoon when everyone was at work or the market. He'd have been attacked for certain. Well, not necessarily for certain, Cecile thought, beginning to walk back to the room she shared with her brother. Anyone would think twice before starting a fight with the broad-shouldered Apollo. She knew from her own clumsiness just how muscular he was. Their collision had knocked the wind out of her, but hadn't fazed him in the least.

"Cecile, you are late! I was getting worried," her brother called out from his bed by the window. A thin ray of sunlight streamed across his worn plaid blanket. He looked exceedingly thin and pale in the light. The winter had not been kind to him.

Cecile rushed to him, excited to share her news. "Etienne, you will not guess what delayed me." She told him the story of the golden stranger and showed him the money. "We can afford your medicines. You'll get well faster now and soon be back to your old self. Maybe we can save some of it for a trip to the country," Cecile fantasized out loud. The money would not last. If she could save any of it, it would be saved to weather another winter. The last winter had not been kind to them. She was lucky Etienne was still with her. Pneumonia had laid waste to his undernourished young body. She too was still overly thin despite the scraps she scavenged from the general's table.

Etienne smiled wanly and sank back against his nearly flat pillows. "I am glad. I think the sun helps." He gestured to the thin stream of light.

Cecile was torn with guilt. She long believed city living had sapped her brother's strength with its pollution, but he was all she had left of family. She could not bear to let him go. She bit her lip, staring at the treasure she'd laid out on Etienne's bed. She did not know when she'd have such a sum at her disposal again. "Etienne, perhaps it is time you went to the country. You could take the money to pay for your keep. There are still families in our old village who know us. You could stay with one of them."

"I will get better, *ma cherie*. We needn't be separated just yet." Etienne replied bravely. "What we need to do, is find a safe place to hide the money, then you need to eat a little and be off to work. I fixed soup from the leftovers. It's on the hob." Etienne nodded proudly to the small black kettle hanging over their fireplace.

"You shouldn't have taxed yourself." Cecile scolded lightly. She stood in the center of their room, hands on hips, looking around. "You've swept and cleaned too. No wonder you look so wan." She shook her finger at him. "You were worrying me. I feared a relapse."

"I am getting stronger every day. I promise you." Etienne beamed under his sister's attention.

Cecile drew her bow across the four strings of her violin in a defiant flourish, bringing her final piece of the evening, a wild caprice, to an end. She glanced at her employer, General Motrineau, and breathed a small sigh of relief. From the size of the grin he wore, he was well-pleased tonight. He and the others at the table broke into applause. Cecile gave a curtsy and made to leave, wishing tonight would be one of the nights the general didn't invite her to sit with them. She detested those nights. It was decadent enough that she performed for his all male supper parties with his fellow generals. The general knew well enough that a proper musicale involved wives and was held in a conservatory or music room, not at the table while men drank and smoked cigars.

"Cecile, ma cherie, come and join us." The general hailed her before she could escape. He motioned to the chair next to him, for which Cecile was thankful. At least she wouldn't have to deflect the amorous advances of his friends.

"I do believe your violinist, Motrineau, plays as well

as Paganini." One of the generals, a paunchy middle-aged man, said further down the table. "I had the pleasure to hear Paganini in Italy when I was there last year."

A man near Cecile laughed heartily. "General Motrineau's violinist is certainly prettier." He turned to Cecile while paying her the lavish compliment. She blushed and stared fixedly at her folded hands. This was the kind of talk she wanted to avoid.

"Better paid too," another put in, "from the looks of that gown, she is obligated to be good." The whole table broke into manly guffaws at the coarse innuendo. She was used to such brash speculation. That didn't mean her cheeks weren't burning. All the guests she played for assumed she was also General Motrineau's mistress. While he had indicated several times he was interested in such an arrangement, she was not. It was bad enough he insisted on dressing her in lavish silk gowns and having a lady's maid do her hair up each evening.

"Gentlemen! Remember your manners," General Motrineau reprimanded the group. He turned to Cecile. "Ma cherie, I have not heard the last piece you played before. Tell us about it."

Cecile spoke hesitantly at first, then more rapidly, losing herself in the description of the caprice and the emotions represented by the runs. It wasn't until she finished that she realized the table had come to full, enrapt attention. No one had filled up a glass or drank from one for fear of missing a single word.

General Motrineau broke the astonished silence. "There, gentlemen, and to think Napoleon is against educating women!" Everyone laughed at his daring tongue in cheek. Cecile took the opportunity to make her escape. She pushed back her chair and curtsied to the men, hastening to leave. To her chagrin, the general rose with her.

"If you'll excuse me for a moment, gentlemen, I must have a moment with the lovely Cecile." He offered Cecile his arm and led her from the room. Behind her, she could hear low, whispered, ribald comments.

"This is unseemly, Monsieur General," Cecile said as soon as they were in the corridor of his opulent home.

"Ma petite cherie, it is not unseemly for a man to wish the company of a beautiful woman." Bolder than usual, the general reached a hand to touch her cheek. "You were brilliant tonight." His hand drifted to her neck. Cecile stiffened.

"You're not wearing the little cameo I gave you last week. I thought it would look especially lovely with this dress. I picked out the coral for that reason."

Cecile met his dark gaze directly. "I am sorry to disappoint you. I had to buy food and medicines."

The general's eyebrows quirked upwards. "We could solve your financial crisis with a more permanent arrangement, ma petite. A house in a safe neighborhood, medicines and doctors for your brother, more pretty dresses for you, your own maid and housekeeper. You'd want for nothing." He lowered his voice to a low, seductive tone. "I don't think you'd find me a demanding lover."

"No, thank you. I must go." Cecile smiled politely and fled down the steps, heading to the kitchen and the little dressing room off it where she changed into her gray serge gown. When she was ready, the cook handed her a satchel of leftovers wrapped in flour sacking. Then Cecile drew close the hood of her dark cloak and started the long walk home with the satchel in one hand and her violin case in the other.

It was difficult to find the willpower to walk out into the cold night after the warmth and luxury of the general's home, particularly on nights like this one when the rain drizzled in a fine, soaking mist. She hoped Etienne would have the fire built up in anticipation of her return.

The well lit houses of the New Regime's 'nobility' gave way to the darker slums where families could barely afford food, let alone candles to light the night. The darkness was a stark reminder of why she stalwartly refused the general's repeated offers. Napoleon's new civic order hadn't changed anything for her or people like her. The direct taxes and the more damaging indirect taxes levied to support the military had drained the poor as surely as the earlier regime had.

Napoleon's idea of avoiding the pitfalls of aristocracy had been to institute the Legion of Honour followed later by his creation of imperial titles. The only difference between the old and the new was that the new hierarchy was based on military merit instead of excluding people from nobility based on the criteria of religion or birth. What ensued was the development of a class of wealthy generals like Murat and LeClerc and her own employer General Motrineau. She knew that her employer had accumulated very little personal wealthy before kowtowing to Napoleon in 1804. Since then, he'd acquired the means to buy a chateau in the country and maintain his elaborate house in Paris. He gave fancy dinner parties regularly and hosted military balls. Rumor in the servant's quarters suggested he was worth nine hundred thousand francs. The sum dazzled her. It mocked her excitement over the francs the stranger had given her in the street.

She could have her share of his fortune if she'd just give in. But her father had instilled in her the family motto: *La vérité ou rien,* "The truth or nothing." The truth was more than simply telling the truth. It was living the truth of your convictions through daily choices. There could be no deviation.

Weary and wet, Cecile climbed the steps to her room. Light peeped out from under the doorway. She rejoiced. Etienne had built up the fire. The little room was warm when she entered. One benefit of a small home was that it didn't take as much wood to heat, she reminded herself.

Etienne was still awake, propped up on his pillows, his face glowing and his eyes suspiciously bright. Cecile flew to his side. "Are you well?" She pressed a cold hand against his forehead, searching for fever.

"Of course, silly." Etienne struggled under her fussy ministrations.

Cecile stepped back. "You looked feverish, was all."

"I look excited. I couldn't sleep until I told you the news. Madame Claubert stopped to look in and she told me. The Panchettes are gone. You know, the bakers that used to run the patisserie."

"Gone? How do you mean?"

"They've disappeared, like their cousins did last

month. There's no sign of them. Their clothes are gone too. Do you think the man you met today has anything to do with it?"

Cecile was immediately worried. "You didn't tell Madame Claubert about my encounter did you?"

"No. Madame Claubert is the worst gossip in the neighborhood."

Cecile breathed easier. The New Regime might have abolished the Tribunate and given power to the Senate to protect the people, but there were still plenty of tools at its disposal for oppression. The New Regime didn't tolerate dissent any more readily than the old regime. She'd heard the generals remark at the dinner table once that Napoleon was different than poor Louis XVI, because he didn't make the mistake of standing by and letting the people criticize him. She'd seen what oppression had done to her parents in their old village. She wasn't about to risk trusting anyone with anything that might somehow incriminate her.

Etienne was growing sleepy now that he'd shared his news. He yawned. "CeeCee, since the Panchettes are gone, do you think we might be able to rent their rooms? I remember they had a lovely window on the top floor that let in the sun. We could use some of the extra money."

Cecile pushed back Etienne's mop of dark hair. There were only five years difference in their ages, but she often felt more like his mother than his sister since their parents had been killed three years ago, forcing them to eventually make their way to Paris. She looked at her brother's droopy blue eyes. "Yes, I think that's a fine idea. I'll make inquiries tomorrow."

Cecile went to her own bed across the room and changed into a nightgown. In spite of the day's excitements, sleep came easily. That night she dreamed of a tall, honey-haired man who walked through the city tossing livres behind him like the pied piper. And she followed him.

Chapter Three

Alain paused for a moment, sweating with exertion, his work shirt damp from his labors. He'd spent the bright April morning working beside the bricklayers and watching the foundations of the new buildings rise from the trenches they'd meticulously dug. He turned at the sound of horse hooves clattering on the cobblestones and shielded his eyes against the sun in order to make out the rider.

"Alain! When did you return?" Daniel swung off his horse in a lithe move, his sandy hair tousled from the breeze. "Are the Panchettes safe?"

"We arrived yesterday evening. They are happily rejoined with their family after a mild crossing of the Channel. You see, everything went off without any trouble and I am now the proud employer of not one but two excellent pastry chefs. Care to dine with me tonight and taste my success for yourself?" Alain greeted his friend in high spirits. The mission had gone well. He hadn't expected many problems beyond disguising his British citizenship. The blockade situation between France and England made it impossible to simply sail his yacht across the Channel with the Union Jack flying high.

"Not one thing out of the ordinary?" Daniel queried in disbelief.

"Not one thing." Alain confirmed. Unless one counted the prideful sherry-eyed miss he'd encountered in the street. She was absolutely out of the ordinary with her defiantly tilted chin. The floppy mob cap she wore could not hide the lustrous chestnut curls of her hair. He had been seized with a mad desire to pull off her cap and free her tresses from their confines. He was sure if he did, her hair would fall to her waist in a glorious spill of silky curls. It was not to his credit that he'd dreamed of her ever since their meeting. Alicia had only been dead a month. He owed her memory more devotion than to dream of an unknown French girl whose name he did not know and whom he would never see again.

Daniel gazed at him thoughtfully, causing Alain to shake himself back to the present. "You seem disappointed I don't have tales of derring-do with which to dazzle you."

Daniel clapped him on the shoulder. "I am only glad enough that you don't have such tales to tell. I'll let you get back to work. I have to ride over to Romney this afternoon for a client. I'll call at The Refuge for supper when I get back."

Alain watched Daniel go, envious of his friend's opportunity for a leisurely ride to Romney on such a brilliant spring day. He had managed to arrange for his morning to be taken up with the business of bricklayer, but he could not put off the responsibilities of the estate. He would spend the afternoon poring over ledgers and bills in the estate office. Alain raised his arm, signaling to the foreman that he was leaving. He would treat himself to a stroll down the promenade before going home to The Refuge.

The breeze off the Channel cooled his heated body, drying the splotches of sweat in his shirt. Alain scooped up a handful of pebbles as he walked and skipped them in the water. On such a clear day, the coastline of France was visible. Only twelve miles separated France from where he stood.

Unbidden, his thoughts dared to drift towards the enticing stranger from the streets. What was she doing now? Was she spending the money on useful items? Was she saving it? Had she squandered the francs on a fancy new gown and girlish fallals? He hoped she would spend it prodigiously. He'd discerned she had great need of it. He'd witnessed the fleeting struggle she'd had with herself over trading the money for information about the Panchettes. Her pride and integrity had won. Those were the qualities that impressed him most, beyond the rich brown pools of her eyes and the pearly translucence of her skin.

His conscience nagged at him for thinking of her at all. Alain threw the last pebble and headed back towards High Street. From High Street, the town rose in a pleasant hodgepodge of houses and shops. The tower of St. Leonard's church halfway up the hill drew his attention. He resolved to stop and say a prayer to quiet his heart.

The interior of the church was dim and soothing.

Alain ran his hand over the smooth stones of the arches. The church had been built in Norman times under the edict that every town must have a stone church. The church had lasted for centuries. Alain sank into a polished wooden pew. He hoped his resort would last half that long. He hoped people would come to it to escape the rigors of everyday life.

He fervently believed that all people needed time to discover themselves beyond the drudgery of daily routines. The advent of the new world would make that possible by creating machines that used time more efficiently than manual labor. People would be free to do something besides work. They'd be able to spend time educating themselves and studying their world through travel and books. They would come to Hythe and have the summer adventures he'd had with his friends, roaming the hills or swimming in a river. What would the French girl think of his grand vision for the future? Would she enjoy hiking through his hills and splashing in his rivers or would she, like Alicia, shun such boisterousness for more sedate activities?

That was patently unfair, Alain reprimanded himself. He didn't even know the girl and he was constructing a personality about her. It should not be a mark against Alicia that she preferred needlepoint and flower arranging to vigorous walking and swimming. It was those delicate qualities that had endeared her to him. He'd grown up with a sister who was all hoyden and horses. Alicia with her fragile brand of gentility was an exquisite novelty to be cherished. Alain knelt swiftly and offered a prayer for the dearly departed.

* * *

"You are the most blessed man in England!" Daniel exclaimed, pushing away from the table and patting his flat stomach. The dessert plate in front of him was nearly devoid of any signs it had held a hefty serving of *pêches et crème gratin.* "I couldn't even tell the peaches were from last year's preserves. I wouldn't have known the difference at all if your chef hadn't sent his regrets."

Alain dabbed at his mouth with a linen napkin, chuckling at the recollection of Armand Panchette fretting over the lack of fresh peaches for the evening's dessert. The good man had been so worked up over wanting to make the dessert special as a thank you for delivering his brother and family safely from France. "I insisted Monsieur Panchette didn't need to put himself out on dessert, but he's a perfectionist and a man who is aware of his obligations. He said it was a matter of honor."

"I'd say he upheld his honor quite well."

A knock on the dining room door interrupted their conversation. Harker entered, looking somewhat put out. "The monsieurs Panchette would like a word with you, my lord." His opinion of interrupting the baron at dinner was evident in his tone.

"Send them in. I'll be glad to speak with them," Alain said, willing to overlook the oddness of the request in light of it being Armand's brother's first night here. He expected the brother, Arnaud, wanted to thank him more formally, although he had told Arnaud earlier it was not necessary.

The two brothers entered. Armand still wore his huge white apron. Arnaud twisted a cap nervously in his hands. Armand's son, Gascon, followed. The two men bobbed and nodded until Gascon stepped forward.

"My lord, my father and uncle wish me to speak for them since their English is poor," he began, waiting for Alain's permission before continuing. "First, my Uncle Arnaud wishes to thank you again. He is deeply indebted to you. We all are, which is why we hesitate to ask for one more favor." At this, the boy swallowed hard, his overlarge adolescent Adam's apple rising and falling with his efforts.

Alain exchanged a quick look with Daniel. "I cannot promise anything beyond listening to your request, but that I will do gladly."

The boy translated for his father. An animated conversation broke out between the threesome. Finally, the boy turned back to Alain. "My uncle Arnaud's wife has a cousin who has run afoul of some dangerous people in France. He works in the household of a man named General Motrineau in Paris. It would be a great relief to have him here with us. We fear he may be arrested and imprisoned." The boy gave a thoroughly Gallic shrug of the shoulders to indicate the hopelessness of imprisonment.

Alain twirled the stem of his empty wine glass. "I must know more about the situation. Who is this cousin? What is his position in the household? What sort of people has he fallen in with?"

Gascon translated and the men nodded their heads in vigorous agreement. Another lengthy conversation ensued in low, fast voices. Alain's French was good but he couldn't keep pace with the rapid exchange.

"My lord, the man we speak of is Pierre Ramboulet.

He is a secretary for General Motrineau. He has become disillusioned with Napoleon's regime and has fallen in with Les Chevaliers de la Foi, a secret society dedicated to the Bourbons."

Alain gave the boy a quizzing glance. "How does one simply 'fall in' with such a league, if they are indeed secret? How is it that he cannot extricate himself?" Alain found it quite telling that the boy shifted from foot to foot at his questions and turned pleading eyes on his father.

This conversation was not long. "You guess correctly, my lord, that our cousin is not an ordinary member of Les Chevaliers. He moves in the inner circles. Lately, there has been worry that his involvement may have been betrayed to Motrineau, who has Napoleon's ear."

Alain nodded sagely. "You want me to rescue him? This will be much more difficult than simply spiriting away a family of bakers whom no one of note will miss." He spread his hands on the pristine damask table cloth. "You are asking me to abet an individual who is actively committing treason against the French government. This is serious business indeed. I will need to infiltrate the general's home, ascertain said individual, and make arrangements for a discreet departure. If he suspects betrayal, he already knows he is being watched." Alain sighed heavily. "I will think on it." He nodded his dismissal to the Panchettes.

Daniel fairly burst when the door shut behind the family of pastry chefs. "You can't be seriously considering it!"

Alain grimaced. "I hadn't planned on doing such a

thing again but I have to say it was a grand adventure, something to fire the blood. I hate to see a man languishing for his convictions when I could free him."

"Or languish in the cell right next to him," Daniel said cynically.

"Still, Daniel, I can't say that I support the politics of free expression and equality for the masses and do nothing when a man risks imprisonment because he voiced his beliefs."

"The man wants to bring back the Bourbons!" Daniel retaliated hotly. "It's not as if Les Chevaliers want to establish a parliament and have men voting for themselves."

Alain shook his head. "He is still a man with an opinion and he should not be imprisoned because of it, regardless of what it is."

Daniel fell silent in the wake of Alain's convictions. Acknowledgement registered on his face. "Then you've decided. You're going to go?"

Alain's voice was firm when he spoke. "Yes."

There was a new man among the regulars gathered in General Motrineau's drawing room for his evening soiree. Out of the corner of her eye, Cecile caught him staring at her while she tuned her violin. He was younger than the others and exuded a sense of vitality at odds with the stiff reserve of the other men— although the others lost their starchy formality once they'd drank enough wine, Cecile reflected sourly. Their often ribald comments later in the evening bore little resemblance to the serious conversations they conducted on military matters. Tonight she hoped the men would be on their best behaviors. Many had brought their wives.

Cecile laid her violin on the pianoforte bench and smoothed the skirts of her pale blue satin gown. The gown was demurely attractive with its soft ecru lace trim around the sleeves and neck. The general had chosen well, as he always did, when it came to gowning her. He did not dress her in gaudy clothes but in styles that befit a young lady her age. Cecile tugged at the neckline. Despite the general's excellent taste, the cut of the gown revealed the swells of her breasts, and she knew the men would ogle. She couldn't fathom young girls wearing such daring gowns and putting themselves on display.

"Ma cherie, are you ready?" General spoke at her elbow. "Everyone is taking their seats. After your performance, I will take you about. You need not feel awkward. I will keep you by my side all evening."

"Thank you, but that is not necessary, General. I don't need such a reward." Cecile tried to get out of spending a long evening in the general's company. She was tired. She wanted to go home and sleep. There were a hundred errands that needed doing on the morrow.

"*Au contraire*, ma cherie. Everyone will want to meet such a talented young woman." The general tapped her on the nose. "Besides, you may meet someone who could provide you with excellent connections, although I'd be loathe to let you leave. You must consider that Napoleon will not leave me to keep order in Paris forever. Someday I'll be called to the field and unable to use your services."

"As you wish then, Monsieur General," Cecile said

with a gracious nod. "You are kind to consider my welfare."

The general's dark eyes softened. "You know I wish things were different between us, Cecile. I could give you much if you would just take it."

Cecile dropped her gaze to the floor, fighting the urge to fidget under the naked affection evident in his intimate voice and in his gaze. Her employer was not an unattractive man. He was a fit man in his mid-forties, gray just beginning to show in his deep brown hair. And he was kind. But he supported a regime that gave itself airs and pretended to be a new order when it only aped the old. She could not give in to a system that saw her parents killed and her father's business destroyed. She was saved from the general's uncomfortable scrutiny by the approach of the young man she'd noticed earlier.

"General Motrineau, is this the lovely violinist I've heard so much about?" The man's French was formal and perfect, too perfect. He wasn't a Parisian. But that wasn't unusual. She knew Napoleon had troops from all over Europe like the Polish Lancers.

The general was introducing her. Good manners forced her to look at the newcomer. Her perfunctory greeting froze on her lips. The newcomer was none other than the man she'd encountered in the street two months ago. She had not expected to see him again except in her dreams. Her first thought was how handsome he looked in his uniform, the gold buttons on his blue coat shining beneath the light of the general's crystal chandelier, and his white breeches spotless. Her second thought was how right she had been to resist giving him information about the Panchettes. He'd been a soldier in disguise that day. No good could have come of telling him what he wanted to know.

"*Bonsoir,* Monsieur. I am always glad to meet one of the general's friends." Cecile recovered her tongue and dipped a polite curtsy. She was gratified to note he was surprised as well by their chance meeting. Unwilling to prolong the encounter in case he mentioned their previous association, Cecile spoke rapidly, "Monsieur General, I am ready to begin."

Alain found a seat on one of the silk-covered Egyptian-styled sofas lining the room and settled in to listen to the concert. He puzzled over seeing his heroine of the streets in such a sumptuous setting as Motrineau's drawing room with its gilt-trimmed panels and Savonnerie rugs. Yet the general had engaged her in an intimate tete-a-tete which suggested he was well acquainted with her. Alain didn't like to ruminate about just how acquainted the general was with her. He had difficulty believing the indignant creature he'd encountered in the streets that had balked at informing on neighbors would allow herself to become a general's mistress. He discarded the idea quickly, recalling her embarrassment at the intimate attentions the general had shown her. Once he'd noticed her discomfort, he'd come to her aid and interrupted the conversation.

The opening measures of the music drew his attention, and Alain listened enrapt. By the end of her first number, he was convinced she was here tonight because of her musical talent. Liberated as French social life might be, Alain doubted it was so liberated that a high-ranking general like Motrineau would invite his friends to a concert given by his mistress. A sense of relief permeated his body and Alain found he could relax, at least as much as an Englishman disguised as a French soldier can relax in a room full of French officers. He gave his attention fully to the concert, mesmerized by the soft sway of blue satin skirts and the graceful curve of her bare arm as it drew the bow across the strings. She was beautiful, talented, and more mysterious than ever.

The concert ended to sincere applause. Groups on sofas and chairs moved off to take refreshment. Alain noticed Motrineau take the lovely Cecile by the arm and begin to move from group to group, circulating throughout the room. Discreetly, Alain attached himself to the group Motrineau was nearing.

"Your little violinist is a delight, wherever did you find her?" An officer's wife cooed when introductions were made to Alain's group.

Alain was embarrassed for Cecile, knowing it must feel awful to be treated like a prize won at a fair or like a novel trinket acquired in some shop. "May I steal your musician for a walk about the room? I know a little something about playing as well and I wanted her opinion." Alain asked, taking the opportunity to dislodge Cecile from the general's side.

"Of course," the general acquiesced graciously. "You're the new officer from Poland who has come to help with training the new cavalry recruits. If you like violin music that much, I'll see to it that you're invited to supper. I often have Cecile play at my supper parties. It's good for the digestion."

Alain nodded his thanks and tucked Cecile's hand in the crook of his arm. It was a windfall that the general had extended the invitation to visit. Now he had a reason to visit again. It was a stroke of fortune that the visit would involve another chance to see Cecile. If the tenseness of her hand was any indication, she did not view it as a sign of good fortune.

"You don't like me?" Alain queried casually while they walked the perimeter of the drawing room. "I thought you'd be glad of a chance to escape that insipid woman."

Cecile gave a small shrug. "Not glad enough to think I owe you anything."

"Of course not. I did not rescue you to put you under obligation to me. I merely wanted you to myself."

"So you don't know anything about the violin." Cecile's voice was haughty and superior at uncovering his ruse.

"I know I've not heard the instrument played quite as well as I heard tonight."

Cecile cast him a wary glance. "Are all Polish men as glib of tongue as you, Monsieur?"

Alain laughed, the overloud sound drawing stares from nearby couples. "I cannot speak for all Polish men. But I would know why I have earned your scorn."

"And I would know your name before disclosing such information." Cecile retorted.

"My name is Alain Stanislawski." Alain quickly supplied, falling back on the identity he had laboriously created for himself.

Cecile quirked a dark eyebrow. "Alain? Are there many Polish men with French names?"

"My mother was French. Now it is your turn. What have I done for you to dislike me?" They approached a set of French doors leading out onto a veranda. Alain deftly maneuvered through them, seeking the auditory privacy of the balcony. They could be easily seen by the others inside. The general could not reproach him for treating Cecile's reputation lightly.

Cecile disengaged her hand from the young officer's arm. "If you insist on knowing, it is because I cannot abide a liar."

"When have I lied to you? We've only known each other for mere minutes." Alain lowered his voice. "The encounter in the street was hardly long enough for you to start drawing conclusions about my moral fiber." Although he'd drawn plenty of conclusions about hers.

Cecile tipped her chin in the delightful way he was coming to associate with her. "That day in the street you did not tell me you were a soldier. You would have me believe that you were an ordinary man looking for the Panchettes. I am doubly glad now that I know your true identity that I shared nothing with you."

"I assure you, I meant them no harm." He had been about to add 'trust me,' and realized at the last moment how absurd she would find that statement coming from a man whom she believed lied to her to obtain information. Instead, he said, "Why would it matter if I'd been in uniform or not? You work for a soldier."

Cecile gave him a sharp look that said he'd stepped too far. "Monsieur, I must eat and pay my bills like anyone else. It was this or harlotry. If you'll excuse me,

I need to return inside and mingle with the other guests." Cecile pushed past him, her silk skirts shushing against his white breeches, and disappeared inside.

Alain stayed awhile longer making polite conversation with other officers. His efforts to learn everything he could about French military were clearly worthwhile. It had been a divine stroke of luck that the general had been looking for an officer to work with the cavalry. He kept an eye on Cecile, watching her flit from group to group, always careful to avoid his group. A few single officers fawned over her hand. One of them pressed a small box into it when he thought no one was looking. But Alain had been looking and he'd seen it. He thought it might be jewelry.

When it was acceptable to leave, Alain made his farewells to the general and excused himself on the grounds of having exercises in the morning. He headed back to his temporary home on the Rue de Faubourg. The crisp night air cleared his head after the hot drawing room. The evening had been more eventful than he'd anticipated but in the wrong way. He'd not discovered the secretary yet. But he had discovered the delectable Cecile with her sharp tongue. Having found her, Alain was reluctant to let her go without knowing more about her.

Chapter Four

Alain watched the French cavalry troops slowly and somewhat awkwardly conduct their flanking maneuvers in the training arena not far from General Motrineau's mansion. The Prussian officer in charge of training new cavalry for Napoleon's army looked askance at him as if to share Alain's own sentiments about the woeful quality of the French horsemen.

The unsuspecting Major Frederick von Hausman was Alain's superior for the duration of his masquerade. Alain found him to be an amicable orderly man of extensive military background. He'd been brought to Paris because of his experience with the elite Spanish riding school in Vienna. Major Von Hausman's specialty was training horses based on his background with the Lipizzaner in Austria, leaving Alain to specialize in training riders. Fortunately, Alain was very comfortable in the saddle and the French cavalry so very uncomfortable that anything he offered them in terms of riding technique would be of use.

Next to him, Major von Hausman shook his head in despair. "Can they do nothing without trotting? They must at least be able to canter through their maneuvers. Whatever will they do on the battlefield?"

Alain nodded in agreement. "We must find a way to make a success of their strengths. If they can only charge at a trot, then we must recommend to their commanding officers that they only be used in large masses or after the artillery has cleared the way with heavy fire."

Von Hausman stroked his well-groomed graying beard. "There is wisdom in that, Captain. I will make a note of it in my report to General Motrineau. By Jove, I think you're on to something. You're a good thinker and a fine horseman yourself. I've seen you on horseback working with the men. Perhaps you might find a place with the Cuirassiers or the Grenadiers à Cheval? Such intense riding in combat is no doubt appealing to a young man of your obvious talents."

Alain shrugged noncommittally. The Curiassers, also known as the *Gros Frères*, "the Big Brothers," were the heavily armored arm of Napoleon's Grande Armée. They could turn the direction of battle with the weight of their armor alone. The Grenadiers a Cheval were the Imperial Guard, the most elite of Napoleon's mounted forces. "I prefer the Lancers," Alain said with feigned pride.

Von Hausman laughed. "After defeating the British at Albuera, I don't doubt it. Napoleon was so impressed with the Lancers heroic performance he's converted several Dragoon regiments into Lancer regiments. I would like to talk with you some day about Albuera."

"Of course," Alain responded, although he would make sure the day for that discussion never came. He had no more been to Albuera than he had been to Poland. But the Polish Lancer victory had created an easy cover for infiltrating General Motrineau's ranks. He'd been lucky enough to meet the real Captain Stanislawski in a tavern en route to Paris.

Captain Stanislawski was no paragon of manhood. He was a rabble rouser, quick to take offense and quicker to drink. After a few rounds of ale with Alain, the captain had taken exception to a comment made about the military by one of the other patrons. Weapons had been unsheathed, a brawl ensued and when the dust settled, Captain Stanislawksi lay dead. Alain saw the opportunity and took it. He had the uniform, the alibi, and the letter of introduction to General Motrineau's staff. Alain couldn't have planned it any better himself. There was always the concern someone would figure out he didn't speak a word of Polish. Fortunately, Von Hausman didn't either. They both spoke French as a second language, as did most of the military officers he'd encountered.

The major dismissed the troops for the day. Alain had the afternoon to himself. He hurriedly curried his mount and saw him stabled with the other cavalry horses. He cleaned up best he could at the pump in the arena courtyard, washing away the obvious layer of horsey smells and perspiration. A more thorough cleaning could wait until he got back to his lodgings on the Faubourg. He'd change into a fresh uniform and get on with his plans; spending the afternoon attempting to track down the elusive Cecile. He knew he'd see her that night since he'd been invited to the general's for one of his dinner parties. It was a sign of how quickly Alain had risen in General Motrineau's favor that he was being invited to the private supper party. He had not yet been able to find the secretary, but he had plans to unearth the secretary that night, which was why he wanted to see Cecile that afternoon. If his plans went well, he wouldn't have time to devote to Cecile that evening.

"Harker, good to see you," Alain said with relief, gaining the foyer of his temporary residence. It was always a joy to see Harker. The butler had insisted he go with Alain. So had his valet, Cranston, who spoke no French but knew how to turn out a well-dressed gentleman regardless. Alain had consented to bring them both under the condition they keep their mouths shut. He was glad for the decision. Hiring French staff would have been far too risky and it would have been exhausting to be masquerading as Captain Stanislawski day and night.

Their presence also helped keep up the pretense that he was a captain. The house on the Faubourg was comfortable and well appointed, as befit an officer of rank. Captains were expected to purchase their own uniforms and equipment as well as maintain a suitable social lifestyle according to their station in life. For instance, to be a Lancer, one must be a son of a landowner. It would not do for Alain to live in the barracks with only a batman.

"Lay out my clean uniform, Cranston, I hope to

make an afternoon call," Alain instructed. "On second thought, lay out some civilian wear." If he did find Cecile, he didn't want to put her off by reminding her of his association with the military.

The bell on the door jingled when Cecile stepped into the musty little shop. She disliked coming here but there was little choice unless she was willing to walk blocks out of her way to another pawn shop. She had as little time as she had money. Such a consuming walk was not possible when people waited on her. A list of errands she needed to run for the sick and elderly lay securely in the bottom of her basket. She had plenty to do before going to the general's that evening.

"Bonjour, Mademoiselle." The fat, greasy man behind the counter greeted her, his permanent leer evident on his face. He came around the corner of the counter, wiping dirty hands on an apron that was dirtier still. "What can I help you with today? Business must be good for you. This is the second time you've been here the past week and half." He eyed her with overt rapaciousness.

Cecile had deliberately worn her drabbest dress, a fusty brown muslin with not even a bit of lace for trim. The gown was dull and frumpy, doing nothing to hint at the figure beneath it. The dress was not having the effect she desired. She cleared her throat. "Monsieur, I have a lovely brooch I'd like to pawn." With utmost care, Cecile unwrapped the piece of jewelry a young admirer had given her two weeks ago at the general's soiree. The brooch was in the shape of a peacock. Lapis lazuli made up the blue body of the bird. Semi-precious gems made up the elongated fanned tail. A tiny diamond chip served for an eye.

Without being a student of gems, Cecile had recognized immediately the piece was not a mere trinket. The price it would bring would leave something for her to save after she'd helped the others. Putting some money aside had become imperative. She'd saved a very small portion of the stranger's money and she must endeavor to save some of the money from the brooch. The general's talk with her at the soiree had been a stark reminder of the inevitable. He would leave one day and go back to the battlefield. Work was already scarce. Once the military left Paris, jobs would be more difficult to come by. She, like so many, depended on the military presence for all nature of jobs ranging from laundry to tailoring to vending.

The greasy man held the brooch in his grimy palm, hefting its weight. He lifted it to his eye, giving the impression of studying it. Cecile hid a smirk at his posturing. If this fat man with a penchant for lechery knew anything about gems, she was a monkey's uncle.

"This is a nice bauble. I feel generous today; I will give you twelve francs."

Outraged, Cecile snatched the brooch back, managing to avoid contact with his dirty palm. "Twelve francs! That is robbery, Monsieur. Single gems in this piece are worth more than that paltry price."

The bell jingled announcing a new customer. Cecile hastily wrapped the brooch in her handkerchief. With a confidence she didn't feel, she said, "I will take it somewhere else." With luck, he'd take the bait. If not, she'd be wasting precious time walking across town because he'd called her bluff.

Greed glinted in the shopkeeper's beady eyes. "Attendez, Mademoiselle. Perhaps we can strike a bargain."

Radiating false bonhomie, the shopkeeper lumbered forward to greet the newcomer. Cecile kept her back to the customer. These were squalid surroundings and she did not want to be recognized, nor did she want to draw attention. No self-respecting woman visited a pawn shop. This was a place for harlots and the dregs. She refused to be mistaken for either. She had her pride. The customer must be a cut above the usual rabble that came in there from the way the shopkeeper was carrying on. The customer spoke, and Cecile stiffened at the familiar voice.

"Monsieur, please finish with the lady. I am in no hurry."

Captain Stanislawski, the Lancer officer. She would know his perfect French with the imperfect accent anywhere. Cecile couldn't decide if she should pray he recognized her or not. She didn't have time. The handsome officer came to her side before she could make up her mind.

"Mademoiselle, we meet again. *Enchanté.*" He gallantly bowed over her hand. She didn't remember offering it. He must have helped himself to it, Cecile thought as she tried to gather her wits.

Cecile managed a simple, "Good day, Captain."

The captain looked from the shopkeeper to her and gave a deceptively harmless grin. "Is there a problem? Perhaps I can be of some assistance?"

Cecile took a moment to watch the slovenly man squirm when confronted with the impeccable manners of Officer Stanislawski. "Captain Stanislawski, I was just leaving. I had hoped to negotiate a fair trade with him for a brooch but we were unable to come to agreement."

Stanislawski assessed the situation instantly. "My pardon then, it seems nothing can be done here. Mademoiselle, if you will permit me, I can direct you to a jeweler that will give you a fair price."

Cecile fought back a smile as the pawn broker began to sputter apologies. She was prepared to produce the brooch again from her handkerchief when Stanislawski waved away the fat man's overtures. "No need, my good man. I appreciate your willingness to bargain, but not everyone has an eye for stones. I wouldn't want you stuck with a piece you couldn't sell." From the arch of Stanislawski's wheat-colored eyebrows, it was clear he thought the brooch would languish in the man's dingy shop for lack of the right appreciative customer. "I bid you adieu." With a gallant flourish, Stanislawski marched her out of the shop into the street.

"Don't stop here," he instructed, tugging her with him. They continued for several blocks until they came to a small grassy park with a bench where they could rest.

Cecile was indignant. "How dare you!"

Stanislawksi was perplexed. "How dare I what? I rescued you from that robber's idea of good business. Isn't that what you wanted?"

Cecile tipped up her chin. "I wanted my money. He was reconsidering his offer when you marched me out the door."

"The offer would never have been fair. Show me the brooch, and I'll get you a fair price. You'll have your money."

Cautiously, so as not to draw undue attention, Cecile brought out the brooch. Stanislawksi whistled in appreciation. "That's a fine piece. I am doubly glad I pulled you out of that shop when I did. Come walk with me. I'll take you to a jeweler. That's the only place you'll get a fair price for something of this value."

"Captain Stanislawski, I cannot go traipsing around the city talking with jewelers. I have errands to run before evening. I have to go to the market, to the patisserie, and the boulangerie," Cecile protested. The man was too handsome and far too confident for his own good.

He appeared to ponder her argument before nodding his head, apparently having made up his mind. "Alright, we'll save time by riding." Without waiting for a response, he hailed a hired town coach and gave the driver the address of a fine jeweler on the Champs Elysées.

Cecile rebelled in the coach. "Monsieur, this is too much! I cannot be seen on such exalted avenues dressed like this!" She held out the worn skirt of her ugly brown muslin.

"Enough with 'monsieur,' 'Captain Stanislawski.' That name is such a mouthful. Call me Alain. As for you being seen in the abominable gown, do not worry. Even if you were dressed in the finest of Parisian fashion, I would not dream of letting a lady conduct the business of selling her jewelry. No gentleman worth his salt would consider it. You shall wait in the coach, and I shall negotiate on your behalf."

"I cannot allow it," Cecile rebutted weakly. When

was the last time anyone had taken up her cause? It was always the other way around. Surely this once she could enjoy the prospect of having her own champion, temporary as it may be. She gave up the struggle, leaning back against the worn squabs of the cheap hackney seats. To her it was complete luxury. She had not ridden anywhere in the longest of times. She could not afford to squander her earnings on carriage rides to and from the general's mansion.

They did not speak again until they arrived at the jeweler's shop, but Cecile could feel his eyes on her. She caught him looking at her once and he only smiled, unbothered by being caught in the act of staring. She couldn't blame him. She spent the carriage ride doing her share of staring as well, only she didn't get caught.

Her hero of the hour was well dressed today. It was the first time she'd seen him dressed as he likely dressed most days. He was not in uniform as he'd been at the dinner. He was not in grubby street attire the day she'd collided with him. He was garbed in finely polished knee-length boots and tan breeches that encased the long legs and muscular thighs of a horseman. His linen was pristine beneath the well cut blue coat he wore. His clothing was not flashy like some Frenchmen, but he was not a Frenchman. He was a visiting soldier from Poland, probably the son of a minor noble.

His clothes were a reminder as to why he could be nothing more than a temporary hero. A noble's son, no matter how minor the title, would not have anything to do with a girl like her beyond dalliance. She was a poor violin player just a few steps removed from homelessness.

The carriage lurched to a stop. Alain made ready to get out. He looked at the brooch one last time. "Cecile, are you sure you want to do this? It is a lovely piece. I am surprised you do not wish to keep it."

That had been her first desire. The brooch was the loveliest piece she'd ever seen. Primly, she clasped her hands in her lap. "I am sure of it. I cannot in good conscience keep the piece when I turned down the offer that went with it." The young officer had hoped to buy affections he could not claim naturally. He had been too prideful to let her return the brooch to him. So she vowed to use it for the benefit of all in her sphere of influence.

Alain was back within twenty minutes, looking smug. "I have succeeded." He deposited an envelope thick with bills in her lap.

Cecile dared a glimpse inside and gasped. "Oh my, I'd never have gotten this price on my own! How did you manage?"

Alain grinned and leaned back, hands clasped behind his head, ready to tell his tale. When he finished, Cecile realized the carriage had stopped. She'd been so caught up in the money and the entertaining story Alain wove, she hadn't thought about where they were going.

"Where are we?" She glanced out the small window, not recognizing the neighborhood. The sidewalks were wider and the people strolling them were better dressed than her haunts. A sneaking suspicion bloomed. This was where her knight in shining armor turned into an ordinary man with nothing on his mind but a quick poke in turn for services rendered. She should have known. She should not have let his clean, golden good looks cloud her usual discernment of human nature.

What man intervenes with a greedy pawn broker, hires a carriage to drive across town, and deigns to sell a piece of jewelry for three times the price she'd have gotten for it, and expect nothing in return? Especially when the lady in question was not even an acquaintance! No man she knew fell into that category. Cecile's cheeks burned. She clutched the envelope, wondering how much of her hard won earnings she'd have to part with to extricate herself from being under obligation to him.

Alain opened the coach door and stepped down, turning back to assist her. "Mademoiselle, I give you, A la Mère de Famille." He made an overly flamboyant sweeping gesture and bowed low.

"Une *épicerie?*" Cecile repeated in disbelief. He had brought her to a grocery store?

"Are you disappointed? I recall you mentioned having shopping to do. This grocer has been in business since the seventeenth century. The store has an excellent reputation. I shop here myself since my lodgings are just a few blocks away."

"The market would be cheaper." Cecile hedged. From the look of the store's well-kept exterior with its fresh coat of yellow paint and its green striped awning, it was expensive.

Alain shrugged, a gesture she was coming to associate with him. "I have an account. I will take care of today's expenses. Get anything you like."

"I have money." Cecile said proudly.

"And I want you to keep that money." Alain reached out and closed her hand around the envelope she brandished. The contact sent a tremor through her. His merest touch inspired confidence in his authority and trust in his judgment. It downright just inspired.

Deciding to trust her instincts that said here was a good man, perhaps the *one* man she might ever meet who wouldn't expect a return on favors received, Cecile stepped into the store. Immediately, the smells of an excellent shop assailed her nostrils: spices, fresh fruits, coffees, and teas.

To his credit, Alain hung back, letting her choose what she wanted and letting her take her time to do it. Rightly, he guessed such an experience was a treat in and of itself for Cecile. He took pleasure in watching her hands run over the fruit like a child at Christmas with a beloved toy. Cecile was a lovely mystery in her drab muslin. Most women he knew would have kept the jewelry; Alicia certainly would have. But Cecile had been adamant about selling it. She had admitted to her moral standards when it came to accepting the gift.

The counter was fast being overtaken by the stacks of her purchases. Alain wondered if she'd thought ahead. He sauntered over to the counter where she stood checking items off her list. Alain picked up a red apple, a smile on his face lest Cecile think he was forbidding her purchases. "Do you think you'll be able to eat all this before it rots?"

"It's not all for me," Cecile said guilelessly. "It's for the neighbors. Madame Andre is too old to get out. Monsieur Pierpoint's rheumatism makes it hard for him to carry his groceries home from market. Madame Boisserie just had a baby and her husband is away fighting in the infantry."

"Stop!" Alain cried in mock dismay.

"Is it too much? I will put some of it back." Cecile worried her lower lip.

The sight of her anxious face touched Alain at his core. "Of course not. I meant it. Get anything you want."

To prove the truth of his word, Alain took her a little further down the street to a *boulangerie* and purchased meat. The last stop was a pharmacy where Cecile bought medicines for cough and fever. The hackney was laden with purchases by the time they were finished. Alain pulled out his pocket watch stifling a curse. The afternoon had fled. It was four o'clock. He had hoped to see Cecile home before his pre-supper appointment with the general.

"Cecile, I regret I must leave you here. I am scheduled to meet with General Motrineau in one hour. I have paid for the hackney. The driver is to take you home." Alain bent over her hand. "I have enjoyed this afternoon immensely. I will see you tonight at the supper, although please understand if I do not wish to call attention to our association. I would not want the general to feel . . ." he'd been going to say "cuckolded" but decided against it. She was clearly not the general's mistress, nor mistress to any other man. "Awkward."

Cecile nodded. "I understand completely." Her tone was slightly chilled. A touch of formality returned.

She was drifting away from him again, becoming more like the defensive young woman he'd sparred with on the general's balcony, and less like the defiant young woman from the pawn shop who mother-ducked her entire neighborhood. He admired the girl he'd glimpsed today. "Cecile, I would like to call on you tomorrow afternoon when I am free from my duties at the military school. We could go to the Tuileries."

"I have things to do. This food must be delivered. There are sick people to tend."

"I'll come with you." Alain offered. "I can carry the baskets," he added, unwilling to be daunted by excuses.

She seemed to think it over, her sherry eyes giving sign of her internal debate. "Alright, meet me at two o'clock at the corner where we collided."

Alain handed her up into the carriage and slapped the side, signaling to the driver. He watched the cab pull into the traffic. She was magnificent. He had not dreamed his violin playing temptress would turn out to be a woman with such a warm heart. Silly as it was to want to tell a stranger about his grand vision of a seaside resort in Hythe, he felt a desire to share that most important plan with her. After seeing her today, he knew she'd feel as he did about creating such a place. He turned down the street for the walk home with a spring in his step that had nothing to do with his impending interview with the general.

Chapter Five

Cecile dressed thoughtfully, if hurriedly, in the little chamber off the kitchen. She'd like to think she'd dressed carefully, but she didn't have the luxury of time to tediously attend to every deliberate detail of her wardrobe for the evening. It had taken longer than she'd anticipated stowing her packages, and her brother had been agog with interest about her afternoon spent in the company of Captain Stanislawski. Alain. They'd become so informal so quickly. She felt she had known him for much longer than an afternoon and that short encounter on the balcony two weeks ago. Perhaps that was why formality was drilled so sternly into young ladies heads. Informality bred a sense of false intimacy.

She peered into the mirror over the washstand and fiddled with her hair, wetting her fingers to twist wispy tendrils into soft, loose curls. Her cheeks were still pleasantly flushed from the brisk walk to the mansion. She would do. Cecile looked down at the deep folds of the gored salmon-colored gown. A white gros-grain ribbon banded the high waist beneath her breasts and complimented the dainty white lace trim on her puffed sleeves. The gown was rich but simple, the perfect choice for a spring dinner held *al fresco.* The arrival of truly warm weather at last had prompted the general to hold this evening's supper out of doors on his magnificent back terrace overlooking a luxurious expanse of lawn so uncommon in the city.

For the occasion, she'd selected several pieces from Vivaldi to commemorate the season. Tonight she would play her violin beneath the stars, circulating amongst the guests. She'd be busy playing, which would leave little opportunity for the general's friends to make spectacle of her and little opportunity to be cornered by Alain. Her heart gave an odd thump at the thought. It was silly to be disappointed by the thought. She'd spent the afternoon with him, and he was coming to call the next afternoon. She'd be spending more time than she needed with him. Secretly, she suspected it would be all too easy to have her head turned by such a handsome man. She could ill afford the complication of a hopeless relationship right now. She had her brother to think of as well as looking ahead to future employment once the general left.

Cecile grabbed up her violin and hurried to the verandah. She took a moment at the glass doors leading outside to appreciate the beautiful spectacle that lay before her. The verandah was decorated with several round, white cloth-covered tables instead of one long table so no guest would have their back to the verdant park. Candles in protective glass shields flickered against the hint of an evening breeze. Further past the verandah's stone balustrade, the trees shone with the light of lanterns, inviting guests to walk the paths. The park had been transformed into a fairy tale complete with champagne-bearing footmen. But not for her, Cecile sternly reminded herself. She was working. Like the livery clad footmen who circumspectly moved among the guests anticipating their every whim, she was part of those who labored to create the fairy tale that lay before her. Cecile tucked the violin beneath her chin and began to stroll among the guests playing a soft minuet.

She caught sight of Alain standing next to the general, talking to a group of men she recognized as General Motrineau's select coterie of friends. Alain had risen fast indeed to be included in such a gathering. He looked resplendent and at ease in his dress uniform, as if he'd been born to such haughty circles. Alain looked her way and she flushed, realizing he'd caught her staring at him. She quickly looked away and moved towards a group of chairs in the park where a collection of officers' wives were gathered beneath a tree.

Talk at the supper tables was taken up by politics and Napoleon as usual, Cecile noted as she stood a decent distance from the tables playing a piece of quiet dinner music. She made it a habit not to listen too closely to what was said in case she inadvertently heard something she should not have been privy to. But tonight, the conversation kept returning to a series of disappearances General Motrineau found intriguing, and Cecile found it difficult to ignore the agitation that ran through the guests.

"If you must know, Captain, I was not completely honest with you this afternoon when you asked for a secretary on loan." Motrineau motioned for a footman to refill his wine glass. "I let you borrow my secretary because I want you to keep him busy, keep an eye on him. I've heard rumors about his involvement in a secret society with royalist sentiments."

Alain did not appear nonplussed by the suggestion. "Perhaps someone wishes him ill and spreads false rumors in hopes of seeing him imprisoned."

Waiting to see that he had all eyes on him, Motrineau continued. "If it is all false, then why have fifteen family members been discovered missing since March? I'll wager they preceded him out of the country. Maybe they are fomenting rebellion abroad and raising expatriates against Napoleon."

Women at the table gasped at such blasphemy. Several guests uttered refrains of "Don't people know they are better off now than they were under the Bourbons?" Cecile wanted to laugh at such uninformed hypocrisy. It mattered little to her if France had a king or an emperor. Her life would not change. Her father had once believed the world could be changed by honest men with honest ideas. He'd ended up dead and his livelihood destroyed.

"It seems they must have had help. They were all bakers by the name of Panchette, of no real consequence to anyone except through their cousin by marriage, my secretary. There was no reason for them to leave unless they were involved in something treasonous." Motrineau spread his hands expansively on the cloth. "So you see, Captain, I must beg your forgiveness for my hidden agenda."

At the mention of the Panchettes, Cecile missed a note, giving the tune a sour sound. The Panchettes! Alain had been looking for them the day they disappeared. She speared Alain with her gaze. What did he know? She missed another note and had difficulty recovering. Had the Panchettes escaped or had they been arrested under suspicions of treason? What role had Alain played in their disappearance? At least she was justified in not telling him their whereabouts. Her glorious afternoon with her gallant prince crumpled against the realities. Alain was a soldier for the regime which had seen her father killed. Quite possibly, Alain had been the one who'd arrested the Panchettes.

Alain gave a familiar shrug and waved away the general's apology. "It is nothing. I shall keep an eye on him." His voice was blasé but Cecile imagined for a moment she'd seen recognition flicker in his green eyes. Speculation ran rife through her mind. Had Alain sought her out today because he hoped to use her to gain access to the neighborhood where they'd met? Was he perhaps still looking for someone else? Maybe his kindnesses today had been calculated measures to gain her trust. Did he already know she was the one who now rented the rooms vacated by the Panchettes? Rooms she was able to rent because of the money he'd given her? The general's loud voice from the table cut through her growing anger.

"I knew I could count on you! You're a fine man, Captain. You must understand I cannot risk having a treasonous viper in my own household. What would Emperor Bonaparte think if he discovered before I did what type of employee I harbored?" The general gestured to Alain's empty glass. "More wine?"

"No, thank you. I've had plenty." Alain declined.

Major von Hausman spoke from across the table. "You're to be commended. You are not who I thought you were. I have to say, I had my concerns about you. None of us knew you by face or by reputation when you were appointed to duty in Paris. Sometimes there are reasons one is sent away on solitary duty from his corps. I feared it was the case with you, Captain, another ne'er do well rich man's son. I asked around through my acquaintances abroad. They'd said you were a drunkard and a rowdy rascal with a tendency for unprovoked violence. I am pleased to report, you're not what they say you are."

Alain looked suitably humbled as glasses were raised in cheers to the new friend in their midst. The general clapped his hands for attention after the impromptu toast. "In honor of our Polish friend, Captain Stanislawski, I have asked my chef to prepare the Polish dessert, Baba au Rhum, made famous in France by King Louis XV's father-in-law, Prince Stanislas Leczinksi." Motrineau made a grand sweeping flourish with his hand, indicating the footmen to step forward with the rum-sprinkled cakes.

As plates emptied of dessert, the diners grew eager to stretch and walk in the warm spring darkness. With permission from the general to enjoy the grounds, the table began to disperse. Suspiciously, Cecile watched Alain lean over and whisper to the general. Moments later, the general beckoned her to his side. "Cecile, our young captain wishes to take a stroll beneath the trees. He is the only one here tonight without a female escort."

Cecile read the implied hint between the lines. "I would be honored to show you the park. The general is blessed with a lovely piece of property in the middle of town; it is not to be missed." She thought her earlier anger was well disguised in her bland conversation.

Alain rose and offered her his arm. A footman came forward to take the violin and safely put it aside. She was loathe to relinquish the instrument, but it would be awkward if not ridiculous to stroll with one hand on a gentleman's arm and the other clutching the neck of a violin.

"You've been shooting daggers at me since supper. What have I done to earn your enmity since we last parted?" Alain asked humorously, guiding Cecile over an exceptionally large tree root in their path. He'd skill-fully maneuvered them out of earshot of the other strolling couples.

"Can you not guess? You seem to be quite adept at subterfuge."

"I am afraid you'll have to explain yourself."

Cecile cast around the grove, making sure of their privacy. "The Panchettes. You were looking for them the day we met and now you've managed to trap their unsuspecting cousin." Her voice was no louder than an angry whisper. The expression of relief on Alain's face increased her irritation as did his next, ill-chosen words.

"Ma petite cherie, is that all?" He even had the au-dacity to follow it up with a laugh.

Cecile pulled away from him and faced him with hands on hips. "Is that all?" She mocked his words.

"Does a man's freedom mean so little to you? A man's life, a family, may be ruined because of your callousness."

Alain swallowed hard. Cecile was gratified her words had hit their target. "Cecile, is that what you think of me? Don't you know me better than that from our afternoon together?"

"The afternoon showed me that rich men are truly alike." Cecile's defenses were on full alert. Alain had not chosen to counter her attacks with denial. She'd provoked him so that he'd tell the truth, the truth she wanted to hear, that he hadn't sent the Panchettes to their doom.

"Pray tell, what is a rich man like?" Alain prompted.

"A rich man tries to buy everything, even people. Do you think I can't see through your ruse? You bought me things, did me favors, and treated me like a real lady in the hopes that I would incriminate my neighbors by giving you an entrée to my neighborhood. What other interest could you have in helping me deliver food to invalids and shut-ins?" Cecile railed. "You got close to me in hopes of being invited in to the homes of the very people you want to investigate."

Alain's voice was forced and low. "First, you are arguing from a position of half-truths overheard at a dinner table. Second, why is it so hard to believe I might share your interest in helping those in need?" He stepped closer to her until there was no distance between them. The white breeches of his uniform rubbed against the light silk of her gown. "Third, when I woo you, you will know it. It will not be with a visit to a jewelers or a grocery but with a visit to my lips to yours. It will bear resemblance to something like this."

Alain tipped her chin up and brought his lips to her mouth, covering it, sealing it with his own. Cecile whimpered more in surprise than resistance, although her conscience briefly argued she should not be kissing this duplicitous man. He had managed to neither tell her truths or lies. At the feel of his strong arm around her, drawing her against him, heat pooled in her stomach.

Cecile gave herself over to the sensations he invoked. His was the body of a man who knew how to protect. How Cecile wanted to believe he'd protect her, that he hadn't used his strength to haul the Panchettes off to a dungeon to await unnecessary justice.

She was embarrassingly breathless when the kiss ended. She still stood within the secure confines of his arms, looking up at green eyes darkened with passion so that now they were the shade of fir trees. "Why did you do that?

"Because I think I've wanted to kiss you since I first saw you." Alain's voice was soft, empty of anger at her accusations. His hand stole up to push a stray curl behind her ear. "You're an enigma, Cecile. Who are you? The spitfire in satin that I see performing in the general's house or the drab dressed Lady Bountiful?"

"I could say the same for you," Cecile retorted, her practical sense being gradually restored. "Who are you? The soldier I see tonight or the man I met in the street." Cecile pursed her lips, suddenly struck by an incongruity. "Whoever you are, I don't know either one of you."

"We shall remedy that tomorrow when I call. We've been apart from the party long enough. Let me take you back."

A footman handed Cecile her violin the moment they stepped back onto the verandah. She took it, grateful to have her hands on something familiar. Playing would help her sort through the jumbled thoughts in her head and give her some distance from Alain. If only Alain would agree.

"Will you show me your violin?" Alain asked, reaching for the instrument in her hands without permission. His own hands were elegant and long, with well cared, short-cut nails. Respectfully, he ran a hand down the body of the violin. The gesture sent a tremor through Cecile. *What would it feel like to have him caress my body in that same manner?* She pushed such wanton thoughts away.

"It was made by a friend of my father, Nicholas Lupot." Cecile said proudly. "But not the varnish, which is my father's contribution to this instrument." She gave a little laugh at her joke, which Alain did not understand. She explained, "Nicholas Lupot makes the most sensational violins. He's one of the premier violin makers in all of Europe. He has a shop here in Paris, I am told. But he's never mastered varnishing. Varnishing was my father's expertise." Cecile ran a hand over the exquisite cherry glossed surface of the violin. "Nicholas uses the harder resins and they give his instruments a cracked look. A good varnish should be with soft resins."

"The violin is a family treasure," Alain commented. "Are you the only one who plays?"

"I am now." Cecile's voice was sharp. She regretted her tone. She couldn't blame Alain for what he didn't know. As an olive branch, she picked up her bow.

"Many people forget how critical the bow is to a quality violin. The violin is nothing without a bow. This is perhaps the real family treasure. It's a bow by Tourte. He is renowned for his inventions on the bow." Her face flushed with enthusiasm. "See how there is varied thickness? Tourte made most of his bows out of pernambuco wood. A true Tourte bow is twenty-seven and nine-sixteenths of an inch. The thick end is four and a half inches long with a diameter of three-eighths of an inch. Then it gets progressively thinner until the head of the bow is only one-eighth inch." Cecile fingered the bow. "He made fancy bows laid with gold; this one is not one of those, but it's still a Tourte."

"Very impressive, you are both a musician and a scholar." Alain complimented her.

"I am afraid I run on too much about the instrument. I hope I haven't bored you."

"On the contrary, I am more intrigued than ever. I have business awaiting me this evening, so I'll bid you bon soir and see you tomorrow afternoon." Alain bent over her hand.

It wasn't until Alain had departed that Cecile realized she'd forgotten to be mad and insist he not call on her. That was what one got for being bowled over by a kiss and a compliment. He'd admired her violin, and all thoughts of whether or not she should associate with a potential scoundrel fled out of her head. Which may have been precisely what he'd intended all along.

Life was getting complicated. Alain had never been so glad to leave a party, or as unwilling. Cecile had been positively entrancing with her sharp retorts. He had not planned on kissing her, but there had been little choice when presented with her tempting defiance in the grove. Her passionate response had been intoxicating, and if he hadn't been so cognizant of the dangers surrounding him in the general's home, he might have dared to take their ardor to its logical conclusion. But danger was stalking him.

The secretary had turned out to be a problem. Pierre Ramboulet had been excited to hear news of his relatives' safe relocation in England, but he'd protested against going with Alain. There were others he wanted Alain to take to safety first, more family members that might be harmed by his disappearance.

Alain did not know how long he could support his identity as Captain Stanislawksi. Major Von Hausman's speculations at dinner had been a crack in the façade. What if Von Hausman contacted his friends and told them his impressions of the Captain? What if a friend of the major's came to visit and inadvertently ran into him? The longer he stayed, the riskier his situation became.

The longer he stayed, the more he'd see of Cecile, who was going to demand the truth from him. The longer he stayed, the more he'd want to tell Cecile the truth as dangerous as that may be. He had no real reason to believe he could trust Cecile with the truth. If events came to a head, Cecile might feel obliged for the sake of her future security to side with her employer. The general had made it clear that traitors would not be tolerated. Motrineau would certainly not tolerate the presence of an English baron in his midst with the express purpose of assisting the person Motrineau wanted to ferret out.

It galled him that Cecile believed him wholly capable of such injustice as arresting the Panchettes. Her distrust of him had been evident in the accusations she'd flung at his head in the grove. He wasn't sure how to convince her that he wasn't a puppet of the New Regime, but perhaps accompanying her on her rounds tomorrow would be a start. In the meanwhile, he had an evacuation to plan.

Alain pushed open the door to his rented home and came to a halt at the sight of Harker's face and wringing hands. Harker was unflappable. Harker never showed signs of distress.

"My lord, we've been invaded!"

Alain became aware of the sound of feet shuffling above him on the second floor. Children's voices cried out in rough play. *Children? Why would children be in my home? Why would anyone be in my home?* No one was supposed to know him.

Harker explained as Alain took the stairs two at a time. "They said they were family of Pierre Ramboulet, that he'd met with you and he told them to come to this address. He told them you'd take them to England, to safety. My lord, I didn't know what to do."

Alain stifled a chuckle at the sight of the disheveled guest room. He imagined the other two guest rooms looked the same. Pallets had been made up on the floor and rag-wrapped bundles containing the family's possessions were piled everywhere. It wasn't exactly funny, but it was certainly comedic. Daniel would have a fit.

"What are we to do?" Harker asked again.

Alain threw up his hands, a smile of consent on his

face. "What can we do? We have to send them to England. Take the boat and go tonight. We can't have anyone suspect they are here." Quickly, Alain summarized the conversation from dinner. "The weather is mild and who knows what kind of weather we may be forced to face if we wait."

"What about you, my lord? Will you come too?" Harker asked worriedly.

"No, I must wait and bring the secretary." Alain tried for levity. "Besides, I have an appointment tomorrow that I cannot break."

"With the young violinist you took shopping today?" Harker eyed him suspiciously.

"She's delightful, Harker. You'd like her."

"I'd like you safely tucked away in Hythe building your city."

Alain laughed away Harker's fears. "I'll be there soon enough. Now, we have people to help and a boat to disguise. I want to make sure someone can sail the boat back here without it being recognized." *Otherwise, I'll be stranded.* Stranded with Cecile. Well, maybe the idea being stranded wasn't so odious after all.

Chapter Six

Cecile tapped her foot impatiently, waiting for Alain
at the appointed street corner. Was he late? Had he forgotten? Had he been detained at work? Had he simply
decided that mingling with the impoverished masses
was not a preferred way to spend a lovely spring afternoon? It seemed forever since the bells of the city had
chimed two o'clock.

She shifted the heavy basket from one arm to the
other. At least she was finding out now what kind of
man Alain Stanislawski truly was. Better this than discovering it after she'd lost her heart to him, which
would be easy to do. A few more days like yesterday
and a few more kisses like the one they'd exchanged in
the general's grove last night, and she'd be done for. It
would be too easy to love Alain, too easy to forget he
was a soldier who fought for a way of life she could not
believe in and that he was from Poland. Some day he'd

go back to his country and resume his life there, most likely as a wealthy man's son with rank and funds. There would be no place in that life for an impoverished violin player.

Cecile scanned the street, shading her eyes against the brightness. Undeterred by her misgivings, her heart raced at the sight of Alain rounding the corner. An odd sense of relief flooded through her at the realization he had not forgotten her. He was merely late. Perhaps he was late because he'd stopped to change clothes. As he neared, Cecile noted his clothes were neat and clean, if a bit worn. They were not the usual attire she was used to seeing him in. How thoughtful of him to dress in a fashion that would not intimidate the people she would visit.

Her cynical side snorted at the naivety of the thought. How intelligent of him not to dress in a manner that would be out of place and put people on edge. He could blend in and cull out information people would otherwise be reluctant to disclose. She'd have to be on watch to see that no one said anything incriminating.

"Cecile, I am late. I apologize," Alain said breathlessly, coming to a stop at her side. From the signs of sweat beginning to form beneath his arms, he'd been running.

Cecile thrust the heavy basket at him. "You can make up for it by carrying this."

He took the basket good-naturedly and fell into stride next to her. "Where to first?"

Cecile pointed to the top floor of a tenement at the end of the block. "We're going to visit Madame Boisserie and her new baby."

"All the way up there?" Alain eyed the building suspiciously.

"All the way up." Cecile confirmed.

The Boisserie home was a typical tenement, dimly lit, cramped, and sparsely furnished. The one luxury, for which Madame must have paid dearly for, was the small hearth built into the wall. She had heat and a means of cooking in her tiny room. Cecile cast a covert glance at Alain to see how he was responding to the squalid surroundings. After dining at the general's, the place must seem the very dregs. To her surprise, Alain didn't flinch. He courteously greeted Madame Boisserie when introduced and plopped the basket down on the room's one table.

"I am going to make you a nice, hearty vegetable soup," Cecile said cheerily, fussing with the woman's bed linens and fluffing pillows. She stooped to admire the baby waving his fists from the makeshift cradle. "The little man is getting bigger every day."

She gave Alain a knife and set him to chopping vegetables while she busied herself around the room with housekeeping. She kept up a constant chatter as she worked.

The very young Madame Boisserie broke into her chatter. "Cecile, you needn't be the one with all the gossip today. I had a visitor earlier. You won't guess what she told me." Without waiting for a response, Madame Boisserie rushed on. "Another family is missing and they're related to the Panchettes."

The chop of Alain's knife seemed louder than necessary. Cecile shot him a distracted look. "Another family? Who could be behind such disappearances?"

Madame Boisserie shook her head. "No one knows, but it's the third family in two months. Either they've been arrested for sordid goings on or they've fled. Do you think we're all in danger?" She reached for her baby and clutched him close. "I don't know what I'd do if someone broke in here." Panic edged her voice.

Cecile recognized the signs of pre-hysteria and quickly intervened. "You have nothing to worry about. The Panchettes are not connected to you." She soothed the woman's fears, reminding her of the connection between the families and the disappearances.

Cecile set the soup to boiling over the hearth and re-packed her basket. They said their good-byes and headed off to the next destination. Everywhere they went, Alain was polite and helpful. When he wasn't slicing bread or pouring milk, he was charming the old ladies, listening to the old men with their tales of by-gone days, or bouncing babes and toddlers on his knee. He played a wild tag game with some older children and patched up a doll for a little girl.

Her neighbors took to him. Alain was a success. He made children laugh, he made stoic old men talk, and he made the old women feel like queens (if the French still believed in queens). Best of all, he didn't probe for unsettling information. Perhaps he didn't have to. At each stop, everyone was full of news about the missing family and Alain quietly soaked it in. Hope-fully, whatever he learned wouldn't prove to be dam-aging, Cecile wished, packing up her basket for the last time.

The basket was considerably lighter now. Its supplies had been dispersed to those who needed them, although the visits had taken longer than usual thanks to Alain's friendliness. Cecile kissed the withered cheeks of Madame Rose and her sister in farewell. To the old ladies delight, Alain followed suit. They tittered and blushed. "Cecile, you keep this one. You won't find nicer manners than this!" Madame Rose instructed, waving them out her scarred door with a gnarled hand. "You two young people run along. Maybe there will be time for a stroll before evening!" She and her sister laughed at their outrageous matchmaking.

Cecile blushed furiously. How embarrassing to have those things said within Alain's hearing. She didn't want him to assume she was falling in love with him. It would make everything between them awkward. It might even drive him away. A painful thought indeed.

"Where to now?" Alain asked when they'd regained the street.

Cecile held up the empty basket. "We're done for today."

"How about that walk? The Tuileries are too far, but I spied a small park a few blocks over." Alain lifted the empty basket off her arm. He swung it experimentally. "Much better! It's not fair for you to carry it now that it weighs nothing. I had to carry it heavy; at least I can have the satisfaction of carrying it empty."

Cecile laughed at his humor. His green eyes sparked with merriment as he teased her. Could he simply make his eyes dance on demand or did they dance all the time? His energy and playful enthusiasm were infectious. Cecile smiled her acceptance and took the arm he offered. Her brother could wait another half hour for dinner. She didn't need to be at the general's until much later that evening. She owed herself a small bit of fun.

The little park was crowded with children enjoying the rare patch of green in the city. A ball rolled across their path, and Alain leaned down to throw it back. "Do you do this every day?" He held up the basket.

"Every day I can." Cecile answered honestly. "I try to bring them all a little something but some days there is less to bring. Today was a good day." She angled her head sideways to see Alain's expression as they walked. What did he think of a woman who worked so closely with the poor? Who was poor herself, or had he realized that yet?

"Does the general know you spend your wages and trinkets on this project of yours?"

Cecile nodded. "He knows I've pawned a piece of two for medicines. I don't think he knows the extent though. It is easy to disguise my plans since he knows I would never keep a piece of jewelry given to me in hopes of winning my favor."

Alain whistled low. "Medicines are expensive. Think what you could afford for yourself if you spent your funds on your needs instead of others."

"I've managed to put a little aside," Cecile said defensively.

"Is that what you did with the money I gave you that day in the street?"

"Some of it. It was March, though, and winter still had us in its grip. Many people in the neighborhood needed medicines."

Alain gave her a soft smile that melted her to her toes. "My kind Cecile, I think you've the most gener-

ous heart I know. I don't think I've ever encountered
such a selfless woman."

The compliment warmed her. Cecile felt her cheeks
flush. "It's the right thing to do."

"No, you don't." Alain interrupted her. "Don't go
saying that it's the right thing and anyone would have
done the same. I know that's not true and so do you.
General Motrineau sits in his fine house, living on an
income largely wrested from foreign coffers and Bonaparte's largesse. He puts more food on the table each
evening than these people see in a month. He is in a
better financial position than you and yet he does nothing." Alain stopped walking and turned to face her, the
amount of passion for his subject evident in his bright
eyes. "You are indeed a most special and unique
woman, Cecile. You see the good you could do in the
world, and you do it."

"What I do is so little. It doesn't even last the night
and people are in need again come morning." Cecile
protested, humbled by the praise he heaped on her. She
didn't make her rounds so that someone would reward
her. She did it because she'd been raised to help others,
because that was what human beings owed one another
out of common courtesy.

"You're wrong, Cecile."

Cecile felt her pulse leap. Alain's passion had a new
focus, her. His eyes had the appearance of molten
emeralds, heated and brilliant. He would kiss her again
if she allowed it. They had not discussed the first kiss.
If she let him kiss her again, what would he think? That
he could kiss her at will? She could not allow more

kisses without knowing the nature of their relationship. It would create false expectations on both their parts. Reluctantly, Cecile stepped back.

"What is it?" Alain looked confused at her rebuff.

"I have to go. People are waiting for me." Cecile improvised a hasty excuse.

"I shall see you home, then." Alain was all correctness, once again the proper captain.

"That's not necessary." If he escorted her home, he might recognize the place as the Panchette's old apartment. If he escorted her home, he would see just how impoverished she was.

"It most certainly is," Alain responded hotly, feeling insulted. "A gentleman should never leave a lady unaccompanied."

"Are you a gentleman, then? And I am a lady, is that what you think?" Cecile asked softly in the late afternoon shadows. She gave a quiet laugh. "We don't know much about each other do we? Too little for there to be kisses between us, don't you think?"

"No, I don't think so." His blunt denial surprised Cecile greatly. "I would gladly learn all I could of you, Cecile. Starting with who is waiting for you at home?"

Cecile grimaced. Her hasty excuse had become a stone around her neck. She could not get out of answering such a simple question. "My brother lives with me. We look out for each other."

"And your parents?" Alain asked, as they walked.

"They're dead," Cecile said in short tones, then continued as if by elaborating she could stop him from asking more questions. "My father was a violin maker in our village south of here. He was imprisoned for speaking out against the emperor. He died in prison and my mother died shortly after of a broken heart."

"My apologies. I hear the reprimand in your voice, Cecile. I shouldn't have pried," Alain squeezed the hand tucked in the crook of his arm.

"Stop here, this is where I live," Cecile said, waiting for his reaction to the shabby building, but as he had all day, Alain showed no sign of repulsion. Instead he began to follow her up the flights of stairs.

Nervously, Cecile gave a squeaky laugh that did her no credit when they reached her door at the top. "You've followed me far enough. I'm sure a gentleman considers his duty is discharged at this point."

Alain ignored her. "Is your brother home? I'd like to meet him."

Cecile had no time to think of a way to deny Alain. She'd wanted to avoid this meeting. She didn't want to answer her brother's questions about Alain, nor did she want Alain to endear himself to her brother. Her brother didn't have many friends, and Alain would leave someday.

"CeeCee, is that you?" The door swung open to reveal her brother, stocking footed and unkempt. He'd probably just awoken from his afternoon nap. "You've brought company! That's fabulous."

Alain took advantage of her brother's exuberant welcome and stepped over the threshold. She'd have the devil's own time trying to get him to leave now. Within minutes, Etienne had engrossed Alain in a game of chess on his battered chess board, one of the small things she'd endeavored to save from their home in the village.

Etienne had taken to Alain just like her neighbors, Cecile thought while wrapping an apron about her waist and setting about preparations for the evening meal. She hoped that the sight of dinner being prepared would subtly encourage Alain to leave. Etienne was way ahead of her.

"Alain, stay for dinner. Cecile's a great chef. She can make anything taste good, even turnips." Etienne's face was bright with excitement over the prospect of a dinner guest. She hadn't the heart to deny him this treat. She hoped Alain could stay. But a man of Alain's stature might have commitments or he might decide he'd had enough poverty to last for one day. No doubt he could do better than the offerings of her meager table. To save her brother's feelings, Cecile tried to soften the blow.

"Etienne, Alain might have dinner plans already," Cecile ventured cautiously.

"Usually I do, but tonight, I am free." Alain pronounced with satisfaction, slapping a hand on his knee. "I thank you for the invitation, Etienne."

Cecile did her best to put a proud meal on the table. She got out the one worn, mended tablecloth to spread on the table. She added a precious dash of salt to the stew and hacked up the extra bit of meat she'd been saving for tomorrow's supper. She cut hearty chunks of brown bread for sopping up the leftover juices.

The meal did not disappoint. Alain ate heartily and complimented the food often. Even if it wasn't the grand fare he was used to, Cecile had offered him her best and she was gratified to see that he had the courtesy to recognize her efforts. She recognized that Alain offered his best as well. He might not have brought a bottle of wine or a bouquet of flowers, but he brought something much better—a vibrant personality that immediately recognized the need Etienne had to make contact with another. Alain told them outrageous stories and made them laugh. It was the best meal she'd eaten in months, including the rich fare she was sometimes invited to sample from the general's table.

Eventually, the evening ended. She had to go to work, and Alain no doubt had other engagements to keep. Cecile walked Alain to the door and stepped out into the dimly lit hallway with him. "Be careful walking down the stairs. They can be tricky in the dark," she warned.

"I'll manage."

Awkward silence ensued.

"Are you making rounds tomorrow?" Alain asked.

"Yes."

"Then I'll come and assist you." His statement left no room for debate. "Thank you for dinner and for sharing your home. Your brother is delightful." His eyes roamed her face. Cecile felt heat pooling in her belly again as it had the prior night under the trees.

"Cecile, do you think we know enough about each other now to permit a kiss?" Alain whispered, his lips an inch from hers. He did not wait for a response, but gently bussed her lips and retreated quietly down the stairs before she could protest. "Adieu, ma cherie, a demain."

"Good-bye my love, until tomorrow." Cecile watched him fade down the wooden steps, his boots clacking into the distance. Her fingers traced her lips, recalling the gentle pressure of his kiss.

"My lord, there are more of them." Cranston's words brought Alain up short as he entered the foyer of his lodgings. There was something highly repetitive about this scene. Running footsteps upstairs confirmed his fears.

"How many relatives do the Panchettes have?" He asked charily.

"That's just it, my lord. They're not related. They've heard through friends that you took some people to safety, to new lives."

"They thought to throw themselves on my mercy, eh?" Alain surmised. "Well, how many are there?"

"Just four, a husband, wife, and two small children."

"I will see what can be done." Alain said briskly, heading to the room that served as his library. "We'll have to keep them hidden until the boat returns."

Alain sank back into the chair behind the broad desk. What had he wrought? He was becoming a regular ferryman, a right dangerous occupation with the cargo he carried—families linked to potentially treasonous individuals. And he still didn't have the secretary. This was more than he'd bargained for. He had come for one man. When he'd assumed the convenient identity of Captain Stanislawski, he had not thought to maintain that identity for more than a week. Now he virtually had a career with the French army. He had not planned on masquerading so deeply, nor had he planned on meeting a woman who appealed to the core of his being with her beauty and her beliefs.

To be honest, he'd taken on the challenge of rescuing the secretary as part of his campaign to hold his grief at bay by filling his life with meaningful tasks. He'd hoped the adventure would keep his wits sharp and his pain deadened. But since he'd met Cecile, he'd never felt so alive.

Chapter Seven

Alain met Cecile the next afternoon as promised and a new chapter of Cecile's life began. The days became magical with Alain by her side. He patiently strolled through the marketplace with her, standing aside as she bought her vegetables and bread. He gallantly visited her coterie of shut-ins, never shirking from offering help or from the dirt of their surroundings. The little room at the top of the stairs vibrated with Alain's presence. Etienne flourished under Alain's attention, regaining the youthful sparkle he'd had before his illness.

Always, Alain was the complete gentleman, thoughtful in his dealings with her friends and with her. He had not offered her money since the day he'd taken her to the grocery on the Faubourg, understanding her need for self-sufficiency. Yet, Cecile knew she had only to ask, and he would provide for her. In that, there was a kind of warm security she had not felt since being under her parents' roof. It lifted a daily burden of worry from her.

For the first time, she had someone to talk to and to confide in. In those days, she talked often about her family and life in the village before the soldiers had come. She talked of her concerns for future employment when the general left Paris, something she had to think through but something she could not share with Etienne, who would worry and push himself to get a job when he was not yet healthy.

The only blemish on their afternoons together was the overt knowledge between them that Alain was courting her. He made no secret of his affections for her, although he did not press another kiss on her since the kiss they'd shared the first night he'd stayed for dinner. Cecile had been wooed by men before. The general's supper table was full of men who thought to buy her affections with expensive gifts. They had all failed. She'd thought herself impervious to Cupid's dart until Alain entered her life. He was wooing her and he was succeeding through the employment of simple kindnesses. How could she fail to be moved by a man who devoted himself to helping the elderly, fixing ragged toys for children, and playing endless games of chess with her brother? How could she not respond to a man who was well-kept and fastidious with his appearance? Clean men were a rare novelty in her world. But Alain was finely turned out, even in the worn clothes he adopted for their afternoon forays. His nails were cut, his jaw shaven, his golden hair neatly trimmed, and his skin smelling faintly of sandalwood.

On occasion when she was particularly struck by his handsomeness, Cecile found herself thinking, *"This is how a gentleman lives, with pressed clothing, colognes, and no doubt a valet to add the right finishing touches."* How wonderful it was to bask in Alain's presence and to pretend for a time that she was a part of his world. He was courting her. Of that there was no question. But to what end? He couldn't marry her, although Cecile liked to indulge her daydreams in pretending it could be otherwise. She didn't think Alain would be so cruel as to ask her to be his mistress. However, she could come up with no other explanation as to why he'd so persistently seek out her company. Her quandary about the direction of their growing relationship threw into sharp relief many difficult realities that made her magical afternoons with Alain no more than that. What did she really know about him?

She would lay awake in bed at night counting off the treasured facts she knew about Captain Alain Stanislawski but the list of facts was short. She knew adjectives—terms that described him. He was compassionate, tender, thoughtful, and she thought, remembering the greasy pawn broker, he was willing to stand up to people who sought to manipulate others. But she knew nothing of him, nothing of his past, his life in Poland, his family or his military career. She had talked much about herself, but Alain had skillfully avoided answering questions about himself in return.

The longer they were together, the more Cecile began to fear the end of their association, for it would inevitably come. If the rumors swirling around the general's dinner table were any indication, the end would come sooner than she might have otherwise expected. Already, the general's suppers were attended by fewer officers, many having been given their orders to march to Napoleon's aid at the front. General Motrineau might have been called to action as well if it hadn't been for a growing conflict of sorts brewing in Paris. Motrineau had been left behind to squelch pockets of rising rebellion associated with a supposed secret society called Les Chevaliers de la Foi and to halt the antics of a phantom menace that went by the name *L'Un,* "The One," who was spiriting dubiously loyal families out of the city.

Cecile made it a habit not to listen to the military gossip at the general's table, but with her livelihood dependent on the general's remaining presence and her growing attachment to Alain, who dined nightly now with Motrineau and Von Hausman, she knew it was in her best interest to stay informed. What she learned, as she discreetly executed a quiet summer lullaby on the violin, sent chills down her spine at odds with the sweaty stickiness of a hot summer night in the city.

The spring had brought victories for the Grande Armée, with Napoleon riding out of the city April 15 to do battle at Lutzen. Dinner talk had been of nothing but the series of victories which followed, victories so intense, the allied forces were suing for an armistice at Pleiswitz by the first week of June. Those had been raucous nights at General Motrineau's table as everyone celebrated. Farewells were exchanged as officers trickled out to join their troops.

Then nothing. The talks surrounding the possible

armistice had brought fighting to a halt, as well as the exodus from the sumptuous lifestyle of Paris. There was no fighting, officers were going nowhere. Just as Cecile wished her idyll with Alain would last indefinitely, she had wished the armistice would succeed and that there'd be no more battles. Then she wouldn't have to look for work. General Motrineau would not be summoned from the city. Now, it appeared that hostilities would resume shortly.

At a dinner in mid-August most of the talk at the table held an underlying current of excitement as officers spoke of departing soon. Some had already begun the task of packing up their households. The future Cecile did not want to face was imminent. At the thought of facing unemployment, a cold knot took up residence in her stomach. She supposed she could always throw herself on Alain's mercy if need be, but their relationship was complicated enough without the added element of pity.

In the next instant, Cecile felt the knot unclench. General Motrineau raised his wineglass. "A toast, to all of you going to seek victory in the name of our emperor! I give you good luck and Godspeed! May we meet around this table next winter, celebrating the conquests of France!"

The men all drank. Glasses were set down and a man near the general spoke. "We haven't heard of your plans, General. Where do you think you'll be assigned?"

The general leaned back in his chair, his hands behind his head. "I'll be here. I've received word that there is battle to be waged in the city."

"An enemy from within!" the man said, aghast at the prospect of such a traitor. Similar exclamations journeyed around the table.

The general motioned them all to silence. "It has come to our attention that for the past several months, a secret society called Les Chevaliers de la Foi has grown more active. They have *bannières* not only in Paris but throughout France. We do not know how militarily disposed they are, but we do know that they have an exacting organizational structure. Their outer circles masquerade as charitable groups; it is how they do their recruiting and woo people to their cause. Their inner circles are very secretive and that is where the plotting against the empire takes place. They have been silent this summer, waiting for the outcome of the armistice, but we have reason to believe they were quite active last winter when it seemed possible the emperor would not recover from the Russian campaign."

The general spread his hands on the cloth. "A secret society alone is of little consequence to the emperor; it is the other part of the scenario that is of concern. There is an individual or group, whom we have dubbed L'Un, who has taken to helping families escape from the city who we believe might be connected to potential members of Les Chevalier's inner circles. Such a concerted effort to protect family members suggests that they may be making ready for a serious strike at the empire. It is my duty to not only break the society but to catch the miscreant who thinks he can challenge the empire with such insubordination." The general's fervor in the form of his fist meeting the table caused the crystal to jump.

There was a clamor of questions. "General, how long has this been going on?"

"Since March, as best we can tell. Perhaps in the excitement of mobilizing the troops for the spring campaigns, this traitor thought to slip past our attention." The general speculated.

Cecile glanced at Alain. Of all the men at the table, he seemed overly quiet. Unlike the others, he was not beside himself with questions or disbelief that someone would dare such a feat under Napoleon's nose. She'd gleaned that the Polish troops were unquestioningly loyal to Napoleon. She would have expected a more explosive response from one of the renowned Lancer captains.

She was surprised to see Alain take his leave of the general shortly after the general invited the men to join him for cards. Alain declined and politely departed without even a glance in her direction. The general had instructed her earlier that he'd not need her once they adjourned for cards, so Cecile quickly packed away her violin and made a swift departure, not stopping to change into her own clothes. Something had disturbed Alain greatly at dinner. He'd been quiet and had had little to offer a conversation that he should have found second nature. No doubt a captain of a squadron was used to receiving orders and packing up or of others doing the same. The surprise could not have been the various orders the men received to report to the front.

Cecile caught sight of Alain further down the street and she followed as rapidly as she could. Still, she could not get within hailing distance. She continued to follow. She saw him turn onto the Faubourg, and then go through a gate in a vined wall that fenced off a house from the street. Cautiously, Cecile pushed open the gate which had remained unlocked. She knew the kind of house that would be behind the wall. It was the kind of house she dreamed of having: three stories tall with shutters on all the windows and lights burning within against the gathering summer darkness.

Voices drifted out to her as she neared the door. She didn't need to sneak, she reminded herself. This was Alain's house, and she was Alain's friend. She couldn't make out what the voices were saying, then she realized creeping closer wouldn't help. The voices weren't speaking French. Alain's was among them, speaking something other than French. It sounded like English, which made so sense at all to Cecile. She could make out none of the words except the startling reference that had her flying back to the gate and out into the street. L'Un.

Blocks away and certain she had not been detected or followed from Alain's, Cecile stopped to catch her breath. She tried to tame her rioting thoughts. Why would Alain be speaking English? Why would he be discussing L'Un with others who spoke English? Suppositions began to form in her mind and the incongruity she couldn't name several weeks ago, became clear. She had collided with Alain in March. But he had not appeared at General Motrineau's house for supper until April. His appearance had coincided with the disappearance of the Panchettes. She found it odd that as an officer, Alain had not immediately been invited to the General's home for a welcome dinner until April when he'd have been in town for nearly a month.

She thought about the insinuations at the table that night regarding L'Un. He was believed to have found his way into the inner social circles of Napoleon's

Paris. Alain certainly had done so. She recalled thinking how amazing it was that Alain had risen so quickly in the general's favor, finding himself a guest at the table any night he cared to lay a claim to an invitation. Lately, he'd been dining there nightly. Was it possible that Alain was L'Un? That he was not a Polish noble's son? The thought was wild and heady, yet sobering. If Alain was not a Polish Lancer captain with a compassionate heart for the poor, then who was he? If what she knew of him was not the truth, then she didn't know him at all. The man she'd spun her romantic fantasies around was nothing more than a fantasy himself. She had fallen in love with a fiction of a man.

Alain paced the back bedroom of the rented residence, pushing his hand through his hair in agitation. The game had escalated without his awareness of it. He had not guessed that there was even a hint of an evacuation effort. He'd been careful to disguise the boat and to obtain French sailing papers so the harbormaster at Calais would not grow suspicious. He'd been careful not to be seen with any of the parties leaving his house. Cranston too could not determine when the breach of security could have occurred.

Of course, Alain knew the security breach was entirely his fault. He'd been so absorbed in his pursuit of Cecile that he hadn't assessed the situation growing in Paris. Alain stopped in front of the window and stared down at the small overgrown garden. If he'd been alert, he would have realized Bonaparte was desperate. The Grande Armée had been rebuilt over the winter in Paris but it had not regained the strength it had known before

the Russian campaign. In March, the German National-
ists had risen up against Napoleon's supporters in Ger-
many. Napoleon and his generals feared a repeat of the
disaster in Russia. Any sign of rebellion at home or
abroad must be put down. Les Chevaliers de Foi must
have sensed the desperation and began hatching their
plans, but they had not been careful enough to avoid de-
tection. The faintest whisper of a plot had been enough
to alert Napoleon's infrastructure.

Such a minor threat would have been negligible if it
had come on the tails of several military victories, but
against the defeats of the winter, the threat was no
longer possible to ignore. Alain should have realized
the politics behind it. An intelligent junior clerk or
aide-de-camp looking for quick promotion would have
detected the commonality all the families had in common. The only stroke of luck was that no one had detected the connection between the Panchettes and
Pierre Ramboulet. Alain hoped that bit of luck would
hold. The Panchettes had left early enough that they
might escape notice altogether. If not, it was not a difficult trail to him. He was new in town. He had shown up
at the time the disappearances began. He had asked to
borrow Pierre Ramboulet to help him with his correspondence. Too many coincidences to be overlooked,
especially if coupled with the random comments made
by Major Von Hausman about how he was nothing like
the man Von Hausman had heard rumor of.

Oh yes, the game had become dangerous indeed. He
did not think General Motrineau would take kindly to
discovering he'd harbored a traitor under his roof. He
would have to leave soon. It was small consolation that

he'd have to leave soon anyway. If the armistice failed, as it looked like it would do, fighting would resume and he'd be expected to rejoin his Lancer unit. Either way, his life in Paris was quickly coming to a head.

The thought would have been more welcome if it hadn't been for Cecile. He was eager to get back to Hythe and see the progress on the resort. The season had officially ended in London, August 12, three days ago. His investors would be visiting Hythe to see the resort taking shape. It would be awkward if he wasn't there. He couldn't expect Daniel to manage them on his own.

The summer moon rose above the trees, golden and warm in the dark sky. Alain scolded himself for spending so much time contemplating the situation when the decision to be made was obvious. There were no viable arguments for staying. He would tell Cranston to pack only their clothes and anything that would give away their English presence. The boat was at Calais. They'd leave the next evening. If Ramboulet refused to go, then he was on his own. Those concerns were easily resolved. More difficult, was what to do about Cecile.

He'd see Cecile tomorrow as planned and ask her and Etienne to come with him. Alain leaned heavily on the window sill and expelled a deep breath. What would Cecile's reaction be to the truth? Would she be able to understand that he was still fundamentally the same man who'd spent the last weeks with her? He just didn't wear a Lancer's uniform. Cecile had no love for the supporters of Bonaparte's regime or soldiers. It had been a token of their growing relationship that she'd been able to put aside her dislike for his uniform. That realization gave his courage a boost. Still, coming with him would be a commitment. She'd be leaving behind her homeland and all that she knew, even her language. To his best knowledge, Cecile might recognize English but she did not understand it. If she agreed to come with him, she and her brother would be entirely his responsibility.

The thought of taking care of Cecile brought a smile to his face. He would love to dress her in fine gowns, finer than the ones she wore at the general's house. She would be an asset to Hythe with her compassion towards others. He would take great pleasure in having her preside over his table and his house. There was only one way he knew of to have a woman like Cecile and that was to marry her. Oddly enough, that was exactly what he wanted to do.

Alain's heart leaped joyously with the realization. He had been foolish not to recognize it earlier. It would not be enough to have Cecile nearby in a cottage in Hythe, to simply see her in passing by chance on High Street or at St. Leonard's. It would be torture to travel to London and leave her behind. He wanted her by his side, sharing the daily living of their lives as they had done here in Paris.

Daniel might say such actions were overly hasty on his part. He had not danced with Cecile or done any of the things a suitor ought to do if he were in London. He had not courtèd her in any of the ways he'd courted Alicia. He'd never taken Cecile for a drive in an open-air carriage, or on a picnic or out riding. He didn't even know if Cecile rode. She probably didn't—an ironic situation for such a neck-or-nothing rider as himself. He'd known Alicia two years before proposing. He'd known Cecile for a few short months. Alain raised his head, struck by a staggering thought. He and Alicia had played the courting game, found each other to their liking, and Alain had taken things to their logical conclusion. He'd proposed to Alicia out of duty. The thought of refusing his suit would never have entered Alicia's mind. Duty demanded that she accept. This was entirely different. He was proposing to Cecile out of love and that would be the only grounds on which she would accept. Alain wondered if she loved him enough to say yes. The rest of his life depended on it.

Chapter Eight

A light summer breeze blew against Cecile's cheek as she lounged on the picnic blanket Alain had spread beneath a tree. Close by, young boys played with toy ships in the park's boat pond. She watched them idly, drinking in the little pleasures of the day. It had been years since she'd indulged in an afternoon picnic and lazed around afterwards on a blanket. Never had she done so with a gentleman, like she did today. She moved her gaze from the boys sailing their boats to the man on the blanket beside her.

Alain lay stretched out, his long legs crossed at the ankles and his hands tucked behind his head. His eyes were closed and he looked utterly at peace in his rest. Looking at him now, it was easy to discard the anxieties of the night, to forget what she'd overheard in his garden. Resting as he was now, it was impossible to believe Alain was other than an officer from a titled family. Aristocracy and athletic grace were mixed in the lines of his reposed body. Only nobility could rest so completely in the middle of the day without a care in the world.

She was somewhat surprised that such tranquil repose came to Alain so easily. When he'd arrived that afternoon, he'd seemed agitated, distracted, as if there was something on his mind. It had seemed odd that Alain had not invited Etienne to join them. He must have understood the broad hints Etienne dropped and he must have known how much Etienne would love a day at the Tuileries.

Alain stirred and popped open one mossy eye with a grin. "You must think me a lazy man, to lay here napping while you pick up our meal." Alain propped himself on one elbow. "Are you tired of sitting? We could take a walk. I have something I wanted to talk over with you."

He said it too casually, Cecile thought, rising to her feet and shaking out her skirt. What could it be that he wanted to talk over with her? Would he ask her to be his mistress? To move to Poland with him when he was recalled? Whatever it was, it was going to alter their relationship. His news would probably do more than alter the relationship, it would most likely end it. Cecile fussed with the picnic basket trying to hide her nervousness, thinking of ways to forestall what came next.

Alain took her hand and tucked it through his arm. "Leave those things; they can wait. I find that I am running out of time."

The cryptic comment sealed Cecile's attention. She spoke frankly. "I have felt all afternoon that you've had something on your mind. Perhaps you should have told me before we picknicked? Then we could have relaxed."

"I wanted to make sure that you had a lovely afternoon. I wasn't certain you would come on the outing if I told you my news first."

Cecile felt a knot growing in her stomach. Her instincts had been right. So much for the lovely food he'd fed her: fresh bread, expensive cheeses, summer fruits and a light red wine. Perhaps they had been part of the bribe he was preparing to offer her.

They walked a bit in silence until they were well away from the usual crowd of others who thought to walk in the park. Alain began to tell her terrible truths, and the fairy tales she'd harbored throughout the summer came to an abrupt close.

"Cecile, I'm not a French soldier."

"Of course you're not. You're Polish," Cecile said desperate to save her fantasies.

"Please, you must not interrupt," Alain cautioned. "I am not Polish, nor am I a solider of any type in Napoleon's army. Captain Stanislawksi is a fiction, at least he is now. He died in a tavern brawl, and I took his papers."

He wasn't a noble-born Pole. There would be no more dreams of being whisked away to a life of minor nobility and ease. But they'd just been dreams. Impossible dreams at that. "Then who are you?"

"I am an English baron. My name is Alain Hartsfield. I am the Baron Wickham."

Her first reaction was concern for him. It was dangerous for an Englishman in Paris these days. Her second reaction was anger. He had lied to her, assumed a false identity and let her believe in it. Checking her anger, Cecile asked, "Why are you telling me this? Surely you know how perilous it is for you to be here."

"I am telling you this because I am L'Un, the one the general talked about at dinner last night. I must leave soon if I am to escape."

"What do you stand to gain with your confession?" Cecile cast an appraising glance at Alain, watching his face for any sign of manipulation. Whatever he wanted of her, it would come next.

Alain stopped walking and turned to face her, his green eyes intent upon her. "I'm telling you these things because I want you and Etienne to come with me. I want to take you to England with me tonight. I'm sorry there isn't more time to think this through, but I can wait no longer without seriously jeopardizing my safety."

"What would I do in England? I don't speak English."

"You'd be my wife, Cecile. I am not simply asking you to come away with me and take a chance in a foreign land, I am asking you to come away with me and be my wife."

Alain still held her hand, and she felt the intensity of his grip until her hand hurt from the pressure. She realized he did not know how tightly he held on. Could it be that he meant it? He wanted to marry her? It sounded too good to be true and it was, she reminded herself, because there was no truth between them.

She drew her eyes away from his handsome face. "Why do you think I will marry you instead of running to General Motrineau with what you've told me? He'd reward me generously."

"Because I care for you, Cecile, and you love me," Alain said quietly.

Cecile's head shot up defiantly. "I fell in love with a fiction. I loved the man I thought you were. As it stands now, I don't know you at all."

"You know my name."

"I know many men's names."

"Cecile, I can understand you're upset, but there isn't time." Alain gripped her forearms in frustration with her resistance. "You know me, only the name is different. I'm still the same man who accompanied you on rounds, who followed you to market, who sat at your table and shared bread with you. Don't let your stubborn pride blind you to those truths."

Tears brimmed in her eyes. In a few moments, they'd spill over and she'd embarrass herself with crying. With her whole being, she wanted to believe Alain's arguments, that he was still the same, that she knew him well enough to trust him with her life and her brother's. But it had been easy enough to assume the identity of Captain Stanislawski. How could she know that he was really a baron? How could she be guaranteed he'd marry her when they left Paris? What if she went with him only to have him cast her aside?

Her lip trembled. "How can I believe you, Alain? If you're truly an English baron, why did you come here at all? How would you have known about the Panchettes?"

"That is a long story, Cecile."

"You must find the time to tell it." Cecile folded her arms across her chest and planted herself firmly in

Alain's path. She was dug in both figuratively and literally.

Alain sighed, recognizing the customary defiance he associated with Cecile. If there was any hope of her coming with him, it lay in telling his tale, how he came to be L'Un. He gestured to a quiet bench out of the way.

"It all began the day I stopped in at The Sail and Oar." Immediately, Cecile's eyebrows shot up and Alain knew that it wouldn't be enough to start there. She wanted to know why he'd been at the pub. Of course she'd want to know. She didn't want to commit herself to a man who drank. But she already knew that didn't she? Hadn't she watched him consume the beverages of the general's table in moderation? Nonetheless, Alain found himself pouring out the whole of the tale, how he'd been in Hythe for the funerals of his parents, how he'd seen the Panchette's boat founder. How the Panchettes had convinced him to rescue the other family members and how they'd told him about Pierre Ramboulet.

She should have been satisfied with his tale, Alain thought when he finished. But something about the shrewd look in her eye suggested she was not. He waited.

"Why would you risk so much for mere strangers? Certainly your need to play the Good Samaritan was assuaged by helping the Panchettes."

Alain smiled at that. "I could say the same of you."

"I'm not the one who is spying in a foreign land."

"My life was empty except for my dream, that someday the world would be a more equal place where people need not live a life of oppressed drudgery simply because they had not been born in better circumstances," Alain said bluntly. He had not meant to say more, but once started, he found he could not stop. Out tumbled the story of his resort in Hythe and his hopes for the little town.

Cecile shook her head. "You're such a grand man. I can't imagine what you see in me, or that someone else hasn't already snatched you up. You don't need a wife like me."

Alain stared at her. "I need a wife I can love." He hadn't thought to tell her about Alicia, he hadn't thought it relevant. But it seemed it was. "I had a fiancée once. She was in the carriage with my parents. She died calling for me. A doctor at the scene confirmed my name was the last one she spoke. I mourned her because I felt that I failed her by not being there that day. For awhile, I confused my grief with guilt. I did not love her."

"Did she love you?" Cecile asked softly, sympathizing with the dead fiancée. She too knew what it was like to love Alain.

Alain shook his head. "I think she loved the idea of me. I suppose it sounds arrogant to say that, but looking back on it all, I can't say I knew that she loved me, unless one counts that it was my name she called at the end." Alain stood up and offered Cecile his hand.

"It's getting late. I have answered your questions. Will you come?"

Cecile rose to stand beside him. "Answer me one more question, Alain. Why do you want to marry me?"

"Why do you think?"

"I think you're a man who takes his responsibilities seriously. While that trait is admirable and rare, I don't wish to wed any man who views me as an obligation. I hope you haven't offered for me because you pity me."

Alain's voice was soft. "I have offered for you, Cecile, because I love you. I thought I had made that clear." He risked a kiss and was rewarded with all the passion they dared express in such a public place.

"Then I'll come." Cecile whispered.

He loved her. He'd lied to her. He'd impersonated a dead man. He loved her. Around and around her thoughts whirled on the walk home, her heart alternating between plummeting disappointment and soaring elation. She could never marry a liar or a man about whom she knew nothing. She would only marry for love, and he loved her. Her carefully constructed criterion was useless. How was she to weigh his love against his lies? Was he the good man she'd seen these past months or a stranger she didn't know?

Her ethical quandary didn't even begin to encompass the risk factors involved in leaving. She'd be aligning herself with a traitor to France. While she had no love for the current regime, she did love her own neck and Etienne's. She'd be at Alain's mercy until she learned the language well enough to interact on her own. She was not used to being so vulnerable. He was a baron, a powerful man. He could do as he pleased with her and she'd have no recourse.

What ifs rose to rebut her fears. What if all he said was true? She would be a baroness. She and Etienne would never be hungry again. There would be hot meals with meat, fine clothes, and shelter. She should risk much to attain such permanent luxuries. If she stayed in Paris, there would be nothing to look forward to except another harsh winter and the struggle to eat and stay warm without compromising herself.

Wasn't going with Alain a compromise of sorts? Her practical self argued. After all, look at the reasons she was considering marrying him. How was escaping with Alain different than taking General Motrineau's offer with exception that Alain's offer came with the veneer of a wedding band? She knew the difference. Alain's offer came with love and it was received with love.

The one unavoidable factor she could no longer overlook was that she loved him. No amount of facts could erase that. She loved the way he played with the children, repairing their toys. She loved the way he flirted with the old ladies and shook hands with the old men. She loved that he did not lower himself to the base behaviors of the other officers at General Motrineau's table. Most of all, she loved the way he looked at her as if he'd lay the world at her feet if he could, like she was . . . her mind groped for the words. Adored. Cherished. Protected. That was why she'd said yes. She would do anything, go anywhere, in order to feel that way again.

She was home. Cecile drew a deep breath and turned the door handle. Etienne looked up from the chess game he'd arranged on his board. Disappointment flitted across his features when realized Alain had not come up.

"I am sorry you could not come on the picnic, Etienne. It was a lovely afternoon, and you would have enjoyed it." Cecile began without preamble. There was no time to warm to the subject. The bells of the city had already tolled five o'clock. "It was important that Alain and I have a chance to talk alone. Alain had something he wanted ask me."

Etienne's face grew animated, his sullen pout fading. "He proposed?" Etienne guessed enthusiastically.

Cecile felt her cheeks blush. She bashfully looked down at her hands. "Yes. He wants to marry me."

Etienne was up instantly from the table, grabbing her hands and swinging her around in a gleeful circle. "This is wonderful news, good enough to be left out of a picnic!" He whooped.

Cecile laughed with him and let herself enjoy the moment. Under other circumstances, it would have been a joyful moment indeed. "Be still, Etienne," she said after a few turns left her dizzy. "It is good news, but there is more that you must hear and you must speak your mind. I am counting on your counsel, dear brother."

Etienne settled back into his chair and waited expectantly. Cecile knelt on the floor in front of him and took his long, thin hands in hers. "Alain has asked us to come away with him. We must leave tonight."

"Go to Poland with him?" Etienne queried. "He's gotten his marching orders, I'd wager."

Cecile shook her head and lowered her voice to a mere whisper. Etienne had to lean down to hear her. "He's an English baron." In the briefest of terms, she related Alain's incredible tale to Etienne. "What do you think we should do? I told him I'd come but perhaps you can see things more clearly than I?" Cecile said when she'd finished her tale. She rocked back on her heels and waited expectantly.

"Do you love him, CeeCee? I mean really love him, and not all the things he can bring us?"

"Yes. It is a frightening feeling. It makes me feel helpless and powerful all at the same time." Cecile rose to her feet and paced the small room, pleating her apron between her fingers as she walked. "When I am with him, I feel I could change the world. He has dreams and he makes them come true. He's building a seaside resort in his town for middle-class families. He believes people should advance in this world on their own merits and not by merit of their accidental birth. He believes all things are possible and when I am with him, I believe it too." Cecile paused for a moment, embarrassed by her sudden burst of passion. "Before I met him, I think I'd begun to lose hope that our lives would ever change, Etienne. Nothing I could do would change our circumstances short of giving into Motrineau's offers."

Etienne nodded his head. "Then I think we should go. All that matters is that he loves you and you love him. I would not have you sell yourself even in marriage to a man you didn't care for. I have been a burden for too long. In our new life, I will find a way to be useful."

Cecile flew to his side. "Oh no, you must not think you've been a burden. If anything, I blame myself for not finding a way to send you to the country. I was too selfish to let you go."

Etienne brushed aside her sentiments. "Enough of the past. When are we to meet him?"

Cecile quickly outlined the plans. She'd go to work as usual. Etienne would spend some of their precious hoard of livres for a hackney to a tavern on the outskirts of town where Alain would be waiting. She would follow the same route. They would await her at the tavern and continue their journey by night in a coach Alain would hire. Instead of sailing out of Calais, they would sail out of Le Havre, a port located one hundred and thirty miles out of Paris. Le Havre was actually forty miles closer to Paris than Calais, but such distances were heady to Cecile. Alain had estimated it would take three days with fast horses to make the trip. Then they'd sail across the Channel and into their new life.

Etienne and Cecile packed very little except for the barest essentials they'd need for the journey. As the bells chimed seven, Cecile hugged her brother. "Be safe and trust no one. Alain does not believe his role in all this has been detected yet, but we must not risk any more than we must. Go quickly after I leave. I will see you soon." Cecile kissed him and hurried down the steps for the last time. She would not be returning the little flat again. The thought was both frightening and elating.

Cecile's caution was not misplaced. The general was in a foul mood, which lifted only slightly upon seeing Cecile. "Ma cherie, I am glad to see you. Wear the lavender gown tonight and play the Vivaldi arrangement I like so much. It may be the only thing that can soothe my temper after the day I've had." He took her hands in his and pressed a kiss to her cheek.

Indeed, the general did look upset. His eyes were tired and his usual immaculate clothes showed signs of wrinkles as if he'd worn them all day. But he gave no indication of what had been bothering him. Curiosity nagged at her. Cecile wanted to ask but since she'd shown no interest in such matters before, she feared it would appear suspiciously out of place for her to do so now. Instead, she changed into the lavender gown and tuned her violin. She would keep her ears open at the dinner table tonight. If the general was troubled, others would be as well.

Cecile played the Vivaldi piece and followed it up with a series of soft French folk songs, hoping to soothe the general's temper. The few guests around the table were tense as well. The sign of so few people invited to dinner suggested the meal was a private affair. For a change, everyone ate in silence. Something must be dreadfully wrong. Finally, the general spoke.

"Gentlemen, there has been good and bad this day. We have captured the traitor from within. It gives me no pleasure to announce that my secretary, Pierre Ramboulet, was a high-ranking member of the secret society, Les Chevaliers de la Foi. We may drink to that." When they had done so, the general continued. "He has been interrogated. We have learned much from him. There was indeed a plot against Napoleon, but I have sent out troops to quell it. I think more than one meeting may be surprised tonight. That is good news. The bad news is that L'Un, who was working to spirit family members out of France, has been revealed to be none other than Captain Alain Stanislawski. Obviously, he was simply impersonating the captain."

The general pulled a letter from inside his coat pocket. "To confirm the false identity, a letter arrived this afternoon to inform me of the captain's death. Apparently, he died in a tavern brawl and this L'Un took his papers, which is why it has taken months for the captain's body to be identified and this letter sent saying that the captain will not be reporting for duty. Stanislawski's residence was empty when my men went over there to arrest him earlier this evening. The place was empty. He has disappeared. We are hunting for him. I am sure we can track him down and when we do, he will hang if he's lucky."

Cecile's mouth went dry. It was all she could do to keep playing as if she'd overheard nothing, certainly nothing that made sense or was of interest to her. Alain was in danger and she'd sent her brother into it as well. She took refuge in the idea that his house had been empty. Had he even gone home after the picnic? It would be hours yet before she could leave the general's.

The men at the table were laughing now over a comment she missed. The general beckoned her to come over. Dutifully she went, pasting on a smile and trying to look as if nothing had upset her.

"Ma Cherie, Cecile, Major Von Hausman recalls that our young traitor had seemed taken with you on several occasions. He thinks perhaps we should ask you if you know his whereabouts."

The family motto, the truth or nothing, ran fleetingly through her head. But the truth would see Alain and her brother dead. She looked down demurely at the hand clutching the violin. "I am sorry, General, if I caused the captain to single out my attentions. It was not my intention to do so. If his interest in me was other than kindness shown to a simple girl, I was unaware of it. I did not see him except for the times he was here."

There, she had lied for him. Hopefully the lies had been convincing.

"There, there, ma cherie." The general patted her hand. "I told you she would know nothing." There was a gleam of triumph in his eyes. Cecile knew she'd answered aright. The general liked the men to think that she was his alone, completely unattainable by others. Clearly, it must be true if she'd turned down the handsome captain's efforts to woo her.

"Go back and play for us. Perhaps your new caprice would fit our mood." The general sent her back to her music.

Cecile gratefully retreated. She had lied for Alain because she loved him, just as Alain had lied for the love of his dreams. It may not make lying right, but perhaps it made it understandable. Suddenly, the world was a crazy place where very little made sense and very little mattered except warning Alain.

Chapter Nine

Darkness closed around her, acting as both blessing and curse while she wended her way through the narrow, curving streets of Paris. Cecile tried to guess what traps might lay ahead. The darkness concealed her but it also hid others. She worried Von Hausman would ask to have her followed. He hadn't been pleased with the general's quick dismissal of her involvement with Alain.

To that end, Cecile was careful to do nothing out of the ordinary. The general knew she didn't squander coin on rides so she refrained from hailing a hackney when she left the general's home. The general would wonder where she'd gotten the extra money, and why she felt it necessary to ride home on this of all nights.

She walked halfway home along her usual streets, trying to stay calm when all she really wanted to do was fly straight away to Alain. Convinced she wasn't being followed, Cecile backtracked to a better part of town where hackneys would be waiting for evening fares.

She hailed one and climbed aboard, giving the driver the name of the tavern. Once inside, she allowed herself to relax. She was safe now. No one knew where she was and there was no reason to guess the hackney bore anyone of consequence to General Motrineau. Then she bolted upright. What if someone asked the cabbie for a description of his passengers? How many fares had the driver had this evening? Would she stand out or had he been so busy that she would blend in? Thanks to her foolishness, the driver also knew exactly where she was going. She should have been more circumspect and asked to be dropped off in a different place. Now the driver could tell the general exactly where she was. How foolish she had been!

From his seat near the tavern door, Alain strained his ears above the din of the pub for the sound of a carriage in the yard outside. Beside him, Etienne cast anxious looks at the door every few moments. Alain placed a hand on Etienne's leg in comfort. "You can do Cecile no good if you raise suspicion. Stop looking at the door. Try to relax and give the impression you're enjoying ale with your favorite uncle." Alain knocked a tankard against Etienne's untouched one and winked.

He was just as nervous about Cecile's safety. There had been a man watching the house that afternoon when he'd come back from the picnic. Discreetly, Alain had detoured and entered the house by the back entrance. Cranston had been ready and they left immediately with no one the wiser. It was likely the man watching the house was a common criminal waiting for a chance to burglarize the house. It was also likely that the man had been sent there to spy on him. Alain could take no chances. Etienne had shown up safely at the tavern around eight o'clock and Alain was glad his departure had been uneventful. Still, he would feel better once Cecile was with him.

"Sir, you love my sister, don't you?" Etienne broke into Alain's thoughts with his nervously asked question.

Alain smiled fondly at the boy. "It is right to protect your sister, although she is more than capable of protecting herself. I am not taking advantage of her if that is what you want to know." He met Etienne's gaze evenly, wanting the boy to see the truth of his love for Cecile. They would both be safe with him. "I'll marry her as soon as she'll permit it once we arrive at my home." He paused, and the conversation lagged. Etienne went back to watching the door. The poor boy was probably unaware of doing it. He would have to be distracted or people would start to remember them.

"Etienne, I have a sister too. Her name is Isabella and she's a year or so younger than me. You will meet her when we get to Hythe. We're very close, she and I."

As hoped for, the subject opened up a flood of questions from Etienne. He was interested in Alain's sister. Alain regaled him with stories of his childhood with Isabella, how they loved to race their ponies on the beach and swim in the coves along the coast. The mention of ponies prompted more questions about Hythe and Alain's home.

"It sounds like a wonderful place!" Etienne exclaimed when Alain paused between tales.

Alain chuckled at Etienne's enthusiasm. "I hope I haven't painted an overly idyllic picture. It's certainly not a center of high society and fashion. The land is rugged, practically carved out of the sea and you must be a strong swimmer just to swim in the sheltered coves." Alain stopped in mid sentence. Had he imagined it or had he heard hooves in the inn yard? Etienne looked to him in expectation.

"Etienne, wait here. I am going outside to use the necessary," Alain winked.

Lanterns lit the yard, outlining the shape of a carriage. Alain strode to the driver. "What have you brought tonight?" He asked convivially.

The driver jerked his thumb at the coach. "A young woman who ought to have more sense than to wander the streets alone so late and frequent taverns," he said gruffly.

The carriage door opened and Alain watched with great relief as Cecile emerged. He hastened to her side and swung her down. Then he reached in his pocket and pulled out coin to pay the driver. Cecile was here and she was safe. Relief flooded through him.

"Come inside, are you hungry?" Alain asked. "Etienne can hardly wait to see you. I think the adventure has made him nervous."

"We should all be nervous." Cecile looked at him sharply. Suddenly, he saw how pale her face was. The hand that clasped his arm was tense with alarm.

"What has happened?" Alain whispered, drawing Cecile into a dark corner of the yard.

"The general knows you are L'Un. He arrested Pierre Ramboulet earlier today, and Ramboulet told him everything."

It all made sense. The man outside his house had indeed been a spy. By now the house had probably been ransacked. He and Cranston had a closer escape than they'd known.

"Alain, they're looking for you. The general has sent out troops to scour the area for you. They suspect you're leaving France." Cecile's voice broke. "What shall we do? The coast will be watched."

"Not if we get there first, and we have the advantage. We know where we're going. They've got to cover all the ports. With luck, the general will have thought to catch me in Paris. He won't have sent out runners to the ports until after he's convinced I've fled Paris. We got a small head start." *And we'll need it.* The general's men would be on horseback. They would travel faster than Alain would with his entourage in a carriage. He and Cranston could ride, but Cecile and Etienne would not be able to keep up.

Alain squeezed Cecile's hand in reassurance. "We'll manage. Go in and see Etienne. We'll leave within the half hour."

Alain called to an ostler to bring around the post chaise he'd leased from the innkeeper. It was small and sturdy. He helped the ostler harness the horses. The horses looked well kept and Alain hoped they had the speed he needed. His plan was to use subterfuge as long as he could by sticking to back roads. They would travel by day and night to cut down on the time they'd be in France. It would help they were headed to Le Havre, but Motrineau would not leave Le Havre unnoticed.

Thirty minutes later, Alain handed Cecile into the post chaise and Etienne scampered in behind her. Alain vaulted into the box and took the reins himself while

Cranston positioned himself on horseback beside the vehicle. With a crack of the reins, Alain set the team in motion. The race had begun.

He drove through the night, putting as much distance between them and Paris as he could. When dawn pinked the sky, Alain's arms ached from their efforts and he knew he needed to stop. Cranston rode ahead and located an abandoned barn. The weathered structure looked perfect to Alain: unobtrusive, plain, and defensible if it came to that. From the hay loft, there would be a commanding view of the countryside. Anyone approaching would be visible with fair warning.

Alain skillfully maneuvered the carriage through the wide barn door, thankful he had a place to hide the conveyance and the horses. The barn would still look abandoned from the outside. He jumped down, grateful for the chance to stretch his legs and shoulders. Etienne and Cecile piled out of the carriage and looked around.

"I hope you're not disappointed." Alain gestured to their surroundings. "I thought it would be safer to avoid inns. Innkeepers have remarkably good memories if they're paid enough. I didn't want the trail to us to be so obvious."

"It's fine," Cecile said optimistically. "Etienne and I are country folk, after all."

Etienne squared his adolescent shoulders. "I slept in the carriage. I'll take first watch," he offered manfully.

Alain hid a smile as Cecile began to protest. He held up a hand to stall her. "Etienne is right. He should take the watch. Cranston and I need to sleep, and you are no doubt still weary from working as well as your flight to the tavern."

Alain reached under the driver's box and pulled out a rifle. "Do you know how to use this?" he asked Etienne.

"No, sir," Etienne replied shamefacedly, casting his eyes down.

"I'll show you. You'll need to fire it if anyone comes our direction." Alain placed a hand on Etienne's arm to steady him and gave him a quick shooting lesson before sending him up to the hayloft.

"He's just a boy," Cecile began when her brother had disappeared up the ladder.

"He's more than a boy. He's on the brink of manhood and has no one to show him how. He can do this, Cecile," Alain admonished softly, coming to take her in his arms and press her close against him. "How are you, my love?"

"I am tired." She yawned into his shirt. "You must be exhausted."

"I'll be fine." It was easy to forget the discomfort in his shoulders and his fatigue with Cecile in his arms. She had come willingly, without protest. He took it as a sign of her trust in him; a heady ambrosia indeed. He would not fail her.

Alain slept for a few hours. When he awoke, a glance at his pocket watch told him it was late morning, time to be on the road again. He stretched and looked around the barn. Cecile's bedding where she'd laid down on a pile of hay with her cloak was empty. A moment of panic struck him. *Had Cecile and Etienne run off? Had she changed her mind?*

Cecile appeared in the doorway, a basket on her arm. Alain's heart began to beat again. "I've been picking berries."

No London belle could have been finer in their satins and silks as Cecile was at that moment, framed in the doorway with the sun streaming in behind her. She was the epitome of the country in summer. She looked utterly divine in her simple work dress and basket, with her chestnut curls falling loose over her shoulders. Her face glowed as if freshly scrubbed, her sherry eyes smiling with a light of their own.

Alain went to her. "If I were a painter, I'd capture your beauty on canvas. You make a most enticing picture." He placed a kiss on her cheek, reveling that he could do such a thing and that soon, he'd be able to do much more. He was her fiancé. This incredible woman would be his wife.

He dug into his pocket. "I forgot to give this to you last night." He opened his hand. A simple gold band lay in his palm.

Cecile looked from the ring to him and back to the ring. Hesitantly, she reached out to touch it with her fingertip. "This wasn't necessary." Her eyes were large and luminous when she looked up at him.

"Yes, it was. You had doubts in the park about the legitimacy of our arrangement. I thought this would serve as a token of my devotion to you." Alain reached for her hand and slipped the band over her knuckle. The ring was only slightly loose. "I have better rings for you at home in Hythe. This one is plain, but it's the best I could arrange in such short notice."

Cecile held her hand up, spreading her fingers and studying the band. "It's absolutely marvelous, Alain. I don't need better. Thank you."

Alain covered her hand with his. "I will marry you as

soon as it can be arranged. I can hardly wait to start our life together. You make me strong, Cecile." Alain lifted her hand to his lips and gently kissed it. He wanted the journey to be over, with all of them safe at Hythe. Most of all, he wanted Cecile to himself. He looked forward to strolling through town with her, showing her the little shops, the beach, St. Leonard's church, and his buildings. But between then and now there were three difficult days on the road and French soldiers to avoid.

The days on the road passed in a surreal blur to Cecile, and she imagined they passed the same way for them all. There was no day or night, only resting and riding. They journeyed most the nights and part of the days, pushing the horses as much as they dared. Alain did not want to risk changing the horses at an inn in case soldiers had passed that way looking for them. To Cecile's way of thinking, she wasn't sure what was worse, pulling into an inn and knowing soldiers were hunting them or not knowing who pursued them. It could be they were pushing themselves for no reason, that soldiers had not been sent in this direction but were instead pursuing phantoms on the Calais road.

Despite the arduous nature of the journey, there were moments of joy. At one rest stop, Cecile played her violin for the little company, weaving a spell of peace against the shadows of their small fire while Alain lounged against a log, his appreciation evident in his dark green gaze.

She took joy too in the continuing bond forming between Alain and Etienne. Alain had been right. Etienne needed male guidance, and Alain was happy to provide it. She knew Etienne would thrive in Alain's household. With that knowledge came the lifting of another worry from her shoulders.

It was a time to reaffirm her faith in Alain. He took time to teach her a few English words during their respites, and he spun endless tales of Hythe for her until she could imagine the town and his home with great detail. She had not been hasty in her choice to follow him. All that he had done confirmed he was a kind man, a man who was desperately in love with her. Never had she dreamed of such feelings as the ones Alain inspired in her.

Early evening on the third day, Alain poked his head inside the carriage. "We've reached the outskirts of Le Havre. There's an inn up ahead. I think we should stop and I'll ask around for news. Then we'll know how to go on."

Cecile glanced at Etienne, excitement flushing her skin. Etienne felt it too. They had almost made it. There had been no trouble so far. They were so close. All they had to do was get to the docks and sail. She grasped Etienne's hand and smiled. The light from the window caught her ring, causing it to shine. "I can almost believe our dreams will come true," Cecile sighed.

"They will, CeeCee," Etienne said without doubt. "Mama and Papa would be so proud if they could see us."

Cecile and Etienne stayed in the carriage, but Alain went about the inn yard with a hat pulled low over his face. He was grimy with road dust. With his battered hat, he was unremarkable in the inn yard except for his height. The yard was alive with a certain aura of excitement. A squad of soldiers had passed through town ahead of them.

They debated their options. They could simply drive the post chaise down to the docks. At least it would keep Cecile hidden from sight in case any of the soldiers recognized her. They could abandon the chaise at the inn and walk to the docks, relying on their ability to blend in with the crowd. They could take horses down to the docks, but that only benefit was in providing them with speed. Chances were, four riders would draw too much attention.

Subterfuge had worked well for them thus far. They elected to simply walk to the docks and slip aboard. Cecile tucked her hair up beneath a floppy mob cap and donned a clean apron from her satchel, doing her best to look like the other nameless women hurrying home to prepare the evening meal. Etienne needed no disguise since the soldiers would not recognize him. In any case, Alain had pointed out that four people in hats might seem a bit overdone.

It was decided that Cranston would board first and tell the captain, a friend of Alain's from Hythe, to get the boat ready to sail. Etienne would follow a few minutes later with a crate of "supplies" on his shoulder, looking the part of cabin boy. Cecile would follow and Alain would board last. Alain reasoned that if anyone was going to be recognized it would be him or possibly Cecile. If the worst happened, at least Etienne and Cranston would be safe.

"Don't even think it!" Cecile cried, clutching Alain's arm in an uncharacteristically weak moment. "I couldn't bear for anything to go wrong."

The other sticking point was Cecile's violin. She and Etienne were willing to leave all but the smallest of bags containing family heirlooms and Cecile's violin with its bow by Tourte. But there was no question of Cecile carrying the violin case. Any soldier worth his pay would notice how odd it appeared for a woman to be carrying the instrument.

"We'll put it in the crate Etienne will carry aboard ship." Alain decided at last, knowing he could not ask Cecile to part from her beloved instrument.

They began their walk to the docks, carefully keeping each other in sight while maintaining a distance between each other so as not to be mistaken for being together. Alain's yacht *The Pride* was in place at the pier. They had spotted a few soldiers in the streets but none had taken notice of them. Down on the docks, it was different. With the onset of the evening tide, boats were making ready to sail. Soldiers were thicker on the docks, boarding ships and checking papers.

Worried about Cranston's inability to speak French, the foursome waited until soldiers had passed *The Pride*. They watched as the captain came up on deck and showed his sailing permissions to an officer. The officer and his assistants left. Cranston walked up the gangplank safely and the little group's hearts soared. Etienne went next, carrying the crate on his shoulder like a common dockhand. The yacht began to slip its moorings as preparations got underway for a quick departure.

"It's your turn, Cecile." Alain motioned to her. "Don't be nervous. I'll be behind you."

Daringly, Cecile reached up to Alain's cheek and kissed him. "I'll see you soon." Her voice gave a telltale tremble. She began to walk. The first ten yards she rationalized her safety to calm her nerves. The soldiers might not even be looking for her. That argument failed. It had been three days. Motrineau must know she was gone by now and he must suspect why. The next ten yards she gave herself encouragement. She was within steps of the gangplank.

A commotion broke out behind her. Soldiers came running down the pier, shouting and gesturing. *"Arrêtez! Arrêtez!* What is your business down here? Where are your papers?" A rough voice barked. At first, she thought they were shouting at her. They were not pointing at her, they were pointing to someone behind her. Fear stopped her progress. Her first thoughts were for Alain. Like Orpheus, she gave a fatal glance backwards.

He was encircled by a ring of soldiers, his hat had fallen off and his golden hair sparked in the twilight. "Papers? Papers?" He feigned ignorance. Cecile watched carefully, attuned to any subtle signal Alain might make. Surely he knew as she did that there was no way he could simply make a mad dash to the gangplank. Even with the preparations for a quick departure, the yacht could not get underway quick enough to avoid being boarded. If he ran, they would all be lost. Their success lay in being able to get underway without suspicion. In a race, they would assuredly lose.

"Monsieurs, my French is not good," Alain said in halting French so unlike the excellent French he spoke with her. "I am Captain Stanislawski of the Polish Lancers."

"Where's your uniform?" A soldier jeered, making a jabbing motion with his bayonet.

"I am on a diplomatic mission, how do you say . . ."

Alain gave a great impression of casting about for the right word . . . *"couvert?"*

"A secret mission?" The apparent leader asked dubiously.

"I say, it is L'Un, the one they're hunting for in Paris." Another spat.

"You're under arrest, for the time being, Monsieur Capitaine. You'll need to come with us until this can all be sorted out."

"I am afraid I cannot go with you." She heard Alain revert to his fluent French and saw him draw his hidden firearm. There was no more benefit in pretending otherwise.

The fool! He could not shoot them all. He needed a diversion, anything that would distract enough of the soldiers so that Alain had a chance of fighting off the remainder. She made a small sign behind her back, motioning the boat to begin to sail out slowly. Any small distance would be an advantage for Alain when the time came. It was going to be a messy getaway. All hopes of subterfuge were gone now. Everything was in the open.

She whispered a prayer that Alain would understand her choice. If either of them could survive this growing debacle of an escape by being left behind, it was her with her connections and citizenship. The alternative was unthinkable. If the soldiers took Alain, he would die by execution. There was no ruse he could fall back on now.

Timing her ploy carefully, Cecile sauntered towards the knot of soldiers. No one stopped her. Most onlookers were fairly distanced from the commotion, hoping to keep themselves from the military's notice. She removed her concealing mob cap and let her curls fall free. Now, instead of hoping the soldiers would not recognize her, she hoped one of them would. She stepped close and screamed, drawing their attention.

She was recognized immediately. "It's the violinist!" a voice cried. It was her cue to run. Cecile picked up her skirts and ran into the twisting streets of town. She didn't run to escape. She had no hope of outrunning the soldiers, but she sought to run long enough to help Alain escape. She knew she wouldn't draw off all the troops, but she'd draw off enough to increase Alain's hopes.

"Cecile!" Alain turned at the sound of her scream. He lunged to break through the circle of his would-be captors once he recognized her plan and saw several of the soldiers set out after her. His lunge brought him up against a brick wall of soldier.

"You're going nowhere." The soldier swung a meaty fist. Alain ducked and retaliated with a swift punch to his gut. The man groaned and fell. Alain kicked him hard, drawing a knife from inside his sack jacket. There were others and Alain fought the remaining men, keeping his back to the wharf and his blade up. He jabbed with his fist and stabbed with his blade, feeling the knife thrust into soft skin on several occasions. He took no glory in it but he could show no quarter. He was fighting for Cecile, for the safety of those on the boat, and for his own life. He could not fall although a knife sliced at his arm, and the sheer number of five to one threatened to overwhelm him.

Desperately, he wanted to search the town for Cecile

but he could hazard a single glance into the streets. Cranston and Etienne shouted to him from the boat. His booted feet were on the planks of the wharf. He sensed the change in surfaces. He discharged his pistol at the closest attacker, taking the man in the shoulder. The soldier fell, slowing down the advance of his remaining comrades. It was enough time to turn and run.

Alain sprinted hard down the remainder of the wharf. The boat had already left its moorings and sailed a safe hundred yards from the pier. Without thought, Alain dove into the cold Channel, going as deep as he dared. The soldiers were not fools. They knew he was not what he claimed. They would shoot into the water in an attempt to catch him. There was no need any longer to take him alive.

The water was cold against the steam of his heated body. His powerful strokes propelled him forward aided by the fight-induced adrenaline coursing through him. Above him, bullets plopped in the water, useless. He judged himself to be halfway to the boat and likely out of range of the military-issued firearms. He surfaced and gasped for air.

Etienne called to him, giving him direction by sound as to where the boat lay. He saw it not far from him. Soldiers on the dock pointed at his head but could do no more. A couple of them were struggling to launch a small craft. Alain struck out for *The Pride* with swift strokes.

At last, he felt Etienne and Cranston haul him onboard. He lay gasping, shivering on the deck. "Cecile, we have to go back for her." He choked through chattering teeth. Cranston threw a gray sailor blanket over him and tried to soothe him. But he would have none of it. "Turn the boat back. We have to go back. We can't leave her there." He protested, tossing his gaze to the stricken Etienne. "Etienne, make them see reason."

Etienne slowly shook his head. "Monsieur Alain, we cannot go back without accepting our deaths and that her sacrifice was useless."

With all his heart, Alain wanted to go after Cecile, but such an action would make her sacrifice worthless. He knew what she wanted. She wanted him safe. She wanted Etienne safe. Etienne could only be safe if Alain lived. Hythe would not be a new life for Etienne without him.

When he could stand, Alain made his way to the railing. He had one more duty to discharge before he could give in to his own grief. Etienne stood at the railing, stoically facing north to England.

"Etienne, I am sorry. I could not save her." Alain began, feeling wholly inadequate at explaining what had happened.

Etienne nodded slowly. "I understand how you feel, but it's what she wanted." With a wisdom beyond his years, he continued. "I think she knew she was the only one who could save you and us. If any of us had been caught, we'd not stand a chance at escaping execution for treason. But she stands a chance, if she can access her connection."

"All the more reason to go back for her, to help her." Alain said through gritted teeth. The thought of his Cecile alone made his stomach clench and his anger rise.

They both knew Cecile would be caught. There was no use pretending she would get away. It was only a matter of what they'd do to her once they caught her. In spite of his grave words, the boy was trying hard not to cry. Alain put his arm around Etienne and pulled him close. "If there's any hope, I'll come back for her. I promise you that I'll risk anything for her."

"Yes, sir. I know you will."

There was no other consolation Alain could offer Etienne. The boy was too old for false hope and Alain's own grief was too great. For all the things he could do, he couldn't save the ones he loved. It was the second time he'd failed them.

Chapter Ten

Spring 1817, Hythe

Spring had come again, and with it, all the familiar longings associated with a world reborn from the old. The spring of 1817 was especially joyful. The long wars with France were over. After spending 1816 worrying about another escape attempt by Napoleon, people were traveling the world again, seeing the wonders the blockades had denied them. Families were reunited. Friends arrived home after long absences. Alain rejoiced over the safe return of his dearest friend, Tristan Moreland, although he found Tristan much changed, or perhaps it was himself who had been altered in Tristan's absence.

It was good to be happy again. In the three years since his own return to Hythe, there had been much sorrow. Isabella's husband died, leaving her a young widow in her mid-twenties, and always there was the pain of losing Cecile.

Occasionally, bursts of happiness could dull the ache of her absence. Tristan's return had sparked a rare visit to London for Alain. He had spent the early season joining his friend in the revels of the capital. He'd rejoiced in seeing Tristan and Isabella marry last spring when her mourning for Westbrooke was complete. Another burst had come from holding his nephew in his arms recently at his christening. But they were bursts of happiness and they were temporary. They could not permanently camouflage the hurt in his heart or fully distract him from second thoughts.

These days Alain's main distraction was provided by his bustling seaside town. His vision for a resort had come to fruition in time to take advantage of the post-war glut of tourists. The hotel was full, the shops on High Street crowded and the collection box at St. Leonard's was brimming with donations left by tourists eager to see the stone church. Arnaud Panchette opened a tea house and bakery that kept his wife and children busy. The others Alain had brought over had found their niches too. One had a tailoring business that rivaled London fashion, and another was an aspiring milliner. Everyone seemed to have landed on their feet. Even Etienne thrived in Hythe.

Now eighteen, Etienne was robust with good health. He swam in the coves and hiked the rocky paths leading from the beach. Alain had hired tutors, and Etienne had learned English with astonishing speed. When he'd completed his course of study, he'd gone to work clerking at the hotel to learn the trade, although Alain had offered to send him to college.

Yes, everyone was thriving in Hythe except for him. It was spring and with all the vigor of his twenty-nine-year-old heart, Alain wanted a family of his own. It was no longer enough to surround himself with the families of others, as much as he loved them. It simply wasn't the same. But a family meant a wife and Alain could not fathom bringing a wife who was not Cecile to The Refuge.

If he'd hoped a young lady would catch his eye during his last sojourn to London, he was disappointed on that account too. No one could rival Cecile. The young girls were too featherbrained, too self-centered, and too lifeless when compared to Cecile's vibrant defiance and generous nature. Alain doubted any of the girls he danced with had ever thought to give up part of what they had in order to make another's life more comfortable. He'd returned to Hythe and devoted himself to the town and the distraction it offered.

Distraction was something he sorely needed. Without it, he knew he'd spend his days wallowing in "what ifs." What if Cecile was alive? That was the biggest "what if" of all. While there had been no word from Cecile to assure him she was alive, there had been no word that she was dead. At first, he'd succumbed to the wisdom of friends like Daniel who said to wait. If Cecile could come to him, she would. After a month and she had not come, the military situation made it impossible to get inside Paris. The great generals had all been defeated and the French were panicking. Napoleon hoped to retreat to Paris and rebuild, which resulted in Waterloo. Europe was a fractured continent of half kingdoms. In the ensuing madness, he would never make it to Paris. He certainly wouldn't make it back out. Nonetheless, it took all his willpower not to sail across the Channel once Etienne was safe on English soil and tear the city apart looking for her.

Perhaps the only reason he hadn't done so anyway was that news had reached him a month after his return that an accomplice of L'Un had been apprehended and executed for treason. The traveler who had brought the tale to Hythe had no more information, although Alain asked numerous questions about the accomplice. Had the accomplice been male or female? What had the accomplice looked like? The traveler knew nothing more.

The news had rent his heart. Most likely it was Cecile whom the traveler spoke of. Alain could think of no other who would fit the description of an accomplice. Only a fool would risk his life after the fact, and he had Etienne to think of now too. He could not risk leaving Etienne alone in the world after he'd already cost the young man his sister.

Occasionally, he'd take down Cecile's violin from where he'd mounted it over the mantel of the fireplace in the music room. He'd caress the hard resin-coated varnish of the instrument and conjure up the countless images he stored of Cecile playing the violin at the general's house. Those days in Paris seemed a lifetime ago.

So Alain stayed in Hythe, tucked away from the rest of the world, working feverishly on the resort and dedicating his life to the benefit of others. He had his daily routine to serve as a buffer between himself and feeling too much pain, just as he had done when his parents had died.

He'd rise early and ride. He'd breakfast and read the five day old newspapers from London. He'd spend the morning in his study attending to business and the afternoon walking the streets of Hythe, overseeing his many projects and visiting with the citizens. Evenings were more difficult since Hythe offered a limited social life, but he managed to fill them with card games, social evenings at the homes of prominent citizens, or with more work in his study.

That April day started the same as any other. Alain dressed in riding clothes and took his early ride amid the sunstreaked morning. The air was crisp with a hint of warmth beneath it. He breakfasted on coffee and an assortment of kippers, eggs, and ham. He reached for the stack of newspapers at his plate, methodically going through each one and circling articles of interest. It was his habit to look for news about investments, political developments, and the goings-on in town. Choosing to be absent from London was no excuse to be ignorant. Alain knew a good businessman needed to keep abreast of all the news. He forced himself to read the society columns to keep up with fashion trends to relay to the tailor on High Street. Occasionally, it humored him to see a friend's name mentioned in the latest *on dit*.

At the bottom of a page in large typeset was an advertisement for a performance at the opera house. Alain's hand stilled. The performance was a violin concert. He concentrated on the headlines of the ad touting the musician as THE PREMIER VIOLINIST IN ALL OF

FRANCE. "Trained by Nicholas Lupot . . ." Alain felt his pulse race. He read on, "once a private musician to one of Napoleon's great generals, she is making her first debut in London, April 16. . . ." *She*. The violinist was a woman. A woman trained by Nicholas Lupot? It was too great a coincidence to be overlooked.

His heart hammering, Alain sprinted through the hall, newspaper clutched in his hand, calling for his horse and then deciding he didn't want to wait for it to be saddled. He ran the entire way to town, not caring about the looks he received from people as he sprinted into the hotel and ran straight up to the desk in the lobby where Etienne sat doing correspondence.

"She's alive!" Alain cried, his loud voice drawing the stares of clients.

Etienne gasped, understanding his meaning at once. "*Mon dieu!* How do you know?"

Alain shoved the crumpled newspaper onto the desk, breathless with his explanation. "It's her, I know it is. How many people could this refer to? There can't be that many violinists trained by Lupot and it's not likely the others are women."

"I can't imagine who it would be if it's not her," Etienne said, his voice tinged with caution. "But it's difficult to hope again after so long. It will hurt all the worse if it's not her. Why hasn't she come before this?"

Alain lowered himself into the chair next to Etienne's desk and ran his hands through his already disheveled hair while Etienne gave voice to the doubts in his mind. The initial euphoria of his discovery faded. *If she had been alive all this time, why hadn't she come to them before now? Three years was a long time to wait*

*without sending any word of her survival. Surely she
knew they would assume she was dead?*

Alain's mind went in dire directions. What if Cecile
had wanted him to assume she was dead? What if she had
changed her mind and hadn't come to them because she
didn't want to marry him? What if she didn't love him?

"There's only one way to find out," Etienne was saying. "You have to go to London for the concert. If it is
Cecile, you will bring her home and we'll all be together again."

Alain knew Etienne was right, and despite his flare
of hope that it was Cecile, he couldn't help but wish
there was an easier way. Suddenly living with the am-
biguous unknowns seemed somehow better than facing
a concrete reality. She either loved him or she didn't. If
she didn't, his life would go on as it had for the past
three years. Except it would be even worse knowing she
was out there and had chosen not to come to him. The
only bolster to his courage was that for the first time he
had a chance to find out the answer to "what if."

The concert was in five days. It didn't leave much
time for second-guessing. Alain would set Cranston to
packing only the basics. He wanted to depart immediately. By carriage, the trip would take three days to
London. He would ride. He had sets of evening clothes
stored at the townhouse after his last dismal visit. He
could purchase whatever else he needed.

Two hours later, Alain swung up onto the back of his
sturdy bay hunter. The hunter was all stamina, and
Alain was counting on every last bit of it. His valise
was strapped to the back of his saddle, and the sun was
high. Alain thanked his stars it was late spring. The

roads would be dry and fast. The road between Hythe and London was long, but Cecile waited for him at the end of it. As he spurred the big horse down the drive leading away from The Refuge, Alain believed for the first time in years that hope did indeed spring eternal.

Chapter Eleven

London, the Royal Opera House

Cecile drew her bow across the violin in a fluid flourish, letting the last note hang in the air, quivering and drawn out with poignancy. Silence permeated the auditorium until the last sound of the note faded away completely, no one willing to break the spell she had woven during the past two hours. Finally, certain there was no more to come, the audience exploded with applause, expelling the collective breath of amazement it had been holding since the moment she'd taken the stage that evening.

A light sheen of sweat glossed her brow as she took her well-deserved bows. She had labored greatly this evening with her varied and extensive repertoire. She had played pieces ranging from the simple but emotive songs of the French countryside, to tear-invoking ballads to classical masterpieces that reminded the audience of her skill, showing off her prowess with a bow and nimble fingers. Tonight, she'd been part gypsy dervish with her country fiddling, and part classical performer. Whatever her music demanded of her, she had given fully with her body. Her shoulders and neck ached from the exertions. She had earned every rose thrown to the stage.

Cecile gracefully bent and scooped up the roses into a makeshift bouquet, knowing how perfectly the flowers complimented the blood red gown she wore. She stood tall, blowing the audience a kiss with her free hand, cradling the roses with the other. Most nights, it did not matter who was in the audience. She couldn't see faces anyway, thanks to the stage lighting. But tonight, she strained her eyes to see. She hoped and dreaded that Alain Hartsfield would be in the audience.

She knew it was a foolish hope. How would Alain know she was coming to London unless he saw one of the ads? Even if he knew, there was no guarantee he'd want to see the concert. Many things could change in three years. She certainly had changed. She was no longer the fresh-faced country girl struggling to survive in a city. Perhaps Alain had married. He was a baron after all. He'd need an heir, and she'd done nothing to assure him that she was well. He had no reason to expect that she was even alive and perhaps every reason to expect that she was dead. What other reason would seem plausible to him?

Her futile perusal of the crowd revealed nothing. Cecile swept another elegant curtsy and exited the stage. She had only enough time to touch up her coiffure and make up before her dressing room door was besieged with well-wishers, all of them male and all of them hoping to entertain the lovely French violinist with a late supper. The guards placed at her door brought in countless bouquets. Cecile consoled herself with the knowledge that at least the poor flower girls standing outside the Royal Opera House were doing a swift business tonight from the looks of the bouquets populating her small chamber. She would go through the cards tomorrow.

The women would send their messages tomorrow, invitations asking her to perform at a private musicale or give a private concert at someone's mansion in town. Her experiences elsewhere in Europe had revealed that she could make more money giving private concerts than she could at large public performances. But the public performance was necessary to draw the needed attention and lay the bait. Everyone would want to hear more, want to claim they had been the first to "discover" the talented woman from Paris. She had money now for dresses, nice hotel rooms and dinners, for traveling expenses, and a highly competent secretary who handled all her business. She had the money now that she and Etienne had craved in Paris.

She told herself she wanted to see Alain if for no other reason than to make contact with Etienne, whom she'd missed desperately since that first evening apart. Certainly, she didn't want to see Alain because she still expected him to marry her. But part of her heart wasn't so easily convinced.

The secretary, an efficient thin woman of unusual height, Mrs. Brown, slipped through the door and slammed it shut with her hip, her arms full of additional flowers. "There is a mob of young bucks outside tonight. You outdid yourself, Madame." Mrs. Brown was English, which made her indispensable to Cecile. Cecile had learned quickly that the English prided themselves on titles. Mrs. Brown insisted on calling her madame although Cecile had insisted it was not necessary or appropriate.

"One gentleman has been quite insistent," Mrs. Brown continued in a tone suggesting the gentleman had quite tried her patience. "He sent you this." She nodded to the small letter resting on top of the bouquets. "I noticed the note bears his seal. This is a titled gentleman." One of the first lessons Mrs. Brown had taught Cecile was the importance of rank, not only of oneself, but of others as well. Many of the men who flocked to her door were young gentlemen hoping to impress her with their father's titles. Few of them had anything more to offer. Those men did not appeal to Cecile in the least. They were simply carousers, interested in sowing wild oats and living on their fathers largesse until they came into their inheritances.

"What is his title?" Cecile asked, her curiosity only moderately pricked. She was interested in one man alone.

Mrs. Brown sighed, somewhat deflated. "He's a baron." Her sigh indicated she thought barons were noble by the skin of their teeth since they were on the bottom of the noble pecking order. But the word baron put Cecile on full alert.

"The baron of what? Does it say his name?" She asked, careful not to let her thoughts run too far afield.

"It looks like Wickham. Yes, it's Baron Wickham."

"Alain," Cecile breathed his name in a heady whis-

per. She sat down hard on the little stool before her vanity. Alain was here. He had come, and he'd come looking for her. "Mrs. Brown, give me his letter and wait for a reply." Cecile extended her hand and took the heavy paper. She broke the red wax wafer and read, her heart pounding.

"Mrs. Brown, tell him I will have dinner with him. Ask him to wait at the theater entrance and then send the dresser to come help me change," Cecile instructed. She had become very good in the past years at issuing orders and taking charge.

With the dresser's help, Cecile readied herself in record time. She changed out of the stunning red performing gown into something more suitable for dinner with a baron. She selected a gown of midnight blue with a satin bodice banded in a wide satin ribbon under her breasts of the same color, falling into a slightly fuller muslin skirt and delicate chiffon overslip. Thanks to her time with General Motrineau, she'd discovered that dressing in gowns made of a single color enhanced her stature. Dressing simply and not giving into furbelows and excessive trimmings gave her an aura of maturity, which her image definitely needed.

Cecile fastened a small strand of Scottish pearls around her neck. They weren't as dazzling as the excellent paste jewels she wore for performances, but they looked elegant and tastefully subdued with the dark dress. She combed out her hair and refashioned it into a smooth chignon at the nape of her neck and snatched up a lightweight spring *pelisse* of silver-gray cashmere. A quick dab of rosewater behind her ears and at her throat completed her toilette.

A look in the mirror before exiting told her she'd accomplished her goal. She wanted Alain to see the woman she'd become, a self-sufficient woman who could take care of herself. He need not be bound to her out of past obligations. He need only to come to her honestly out of the dictates of his heart.

Cecile found Alain waiting outside, leaning his long form against one of the opera house's colonnades. She took a moment to study him from her vantage point. She could not see his face, but his shoulders were as broad as she remembered them, beneath the black opera cloak he wore. He carried a silk top hat and walking stick in one hand, his honey-gold hair glowing like a halo in contrast to the darkness of his attire in the spring evening. Her heart began to race at the prospect of her dream so close to fulfillment.

In her daydreams she had long played out the scene in which she and Alain found each other again. She would be the grand lady, finely dressed, self assured, poised with the manners of the highborn—a woman Alain would be pleased to call his wife, a woman worthy of the title "Lady." All those fantasies spun in the dark loneliness of the years without him were worthless now. She stood rooted on the theater steps, unable to progress or even to find her voice, so moving was the sight of him. Like water to the thirsting, rope to the drowning, fire to the freezing, the sight of him was all that and more.

Cecile found her voice and claimed her dream in a single, soft spoken word. "Alain."

He turned at the summons and Cecile drank in the sight of his face, so familiar and yet slightly altered

from the face that populated her dreams on a regular basis. This face was tanned from hours spent working beneath the sun, but the mossy eyes were still as she recalled. He was dressed impeccably, overwhelmingly breathtaking, as golden, as godlike as she'd ever thought him. Her imagination had not failed her these long years and at the sight of him, she regretted not a single moment of her sacrifice.

"Cecile!"

Her heart skipped at the sound of her name on his lips and all thought of playing the grand lady fled. She cared nothing for decorum, but only to be in his arms again. He was pushing his way up the steps towards her, heedless of the stares his charge drew from the last of the post-theater crowd still mingling on the steps. She could not wait for him to reach her. Cecile lifted the hem of her satin gown and rushed to meet him.

His arms were about her enfolding her in their strength. Cecile breathed the scent of him and turned her face to his. In that moment his lips found hers in a soul-binding kiss, and she knew she was home. His body was all heat and hardness as he pressed her to him, his joy, his happiness complete. Unbidden, the words he'd spoken to her beneath the tree during General Motrineau's al fresco party came to mind. 'When I woo you, you shall know it.' And she did. The man for whom she'd defied an army had waited for her. She had lived for this moment and it had come. As long as she lived, there would not be a moment to rival this one. Her face was wet with her joy when they drew apart, Alain keeping her hands in his as if he could not bear to be separated from her again even if only by inches.

"Cecile, you're a vision. Let me look at you!" Alain spread her arms wide and stepped back, taking in the whole of her. His eyes reflected the truth she'd seen in the mirror.

"Thank you. You look well yourself," she said rather stiffly, still at a loss for words.

"You're speaking English!" Alain exclaimed in wonder. "When did you learn?"

"I took lessons in Paris. It seemed imperative to learn English after . . ." Her voice broke off. She had not meant to discuss the past standing in Covent Garden. Yet, there was so much between them that needed saying, why she hadn't come to him until now. The questions he must have!

Alain understood, a smile of joy wreathing his face. "Say no more. We have so much to discuss. I doubt one night will be enough, but we have time now. Come and dine with me. I've taken a private room at Rules for us."

"Yes." Cecile breathed, her eyes unable to leave his. This was a fairy tale and daydream combined. She was with Alain again, and he was escorting her to dinner in London. It was so far removed from anything she'd dared to dream.

Alain tucked her hand in the crook of his arm. "I have taken a table at Rules for us. It's not far, just across the piazza at Southampton and Maiden Lane. We can walk, if you like."

Cecile found her voice enough to muster a little of the old teasing. "Were you that sure I'd accept your invitation when you sent your card?"

"If you did accept, I could hardly be caught without

having made any preparations. I thought it better to think ahead and risk looking the fool to the proprietor instead of looking the fool with you." Alain admitted honestly.

"You could never look the fool to me, Alain." Cecile said softly, squeezing his arm. "I'd be just as happy with a bottle of wine, cheese in the park, and a loaf of crusty bread."

Alain smiled down at her, "I know. We'll have time for that too. We'll have all the time you will allow me, Cecile."

Rules was indeed close by and their walk was only a matter of a few minutes. Inside, the maitre d' led them straight away to a private room which could have seated six, expressing the whole while how honored they were that a baron and such a renowned violinist would patronize the establishment.

"I hope you don't mind the privacy," Alain said after the gushing maitre d' had left. "I selfishly want you to myself." He broke off suddenly. "My God, Cecile. I can't believe you're here. That we're here, having dinner together. You're alive!" He reached for her hands across the table and stroked their backs with the pads of his thumbs.

"Alain, you'll make me cry." Cecile scolded while the proof of her scold welled in her eyes.

"I know. I feel it too. Tonight is a miracle. Somehow it is hard to concentrate on the ordinary." He smiled and winked. "Nonetheless, I do hear their roebuck venison is excellent."

Cecile laughed, appreciating his efforts at small talk. Such banter would give them time to settle their rampant emotions. She matched his attempt at normal conversation. "Tell me about Rules, Alain. Do you come here often?"

"I haven't been to London much in recent years," Alain shrugged, "Its amusements haven't been all that diverting for me, at least not until tonight." He caressed her hands, lost for a moment. Then he brightened. "But Rules has been in business for eighteen years. It's become a regular spot for theatergoers. I imagine most of the guests tonight were also at your concert, another reason I didn't want to take a public table. I thought you might not like the attention."

Cecile found the small talk flowing between them consoling. It was a wondrous thing to talk with Alain as if it were an everyday occurrence. It was no small triumph to her that she could do so in English. But conversing about roebuck and oysters was far from what she really wanted to ask and no doubt far from the things weighing on Alain's mind.

At last, the entrees arrived and the servers left them alone to dine. For the first time that evening, they had both the privacy and the time they needed for their long awaited discussion.

"How did you learn English?" Alain broached the subject, picking up the reference she'd made in the piazza.

Cecile took a sip of the rich red wine, buying time to organize her thoughts. Where to start? How to start? "I studied violin-making and playing under Nicholas Lupot. Do you remember him? I mentioned him to you before. He has a small but lucrative business in Paris. When I showed talent for the craft and for performing, Monsieur Lupot kindly hired a tutor for me. When I proved proficient in that as well, we hit on the idea of me touring. He has no interest himself in travel, but he is interested in profit and it is good for the rest of the world to see the greatness of France." Cecile paused and took another bite of the venison.

"He found my secretary, Mrs. Brown as well. She used to be a lady's companion. She taught me all types of things about going on in society: how to dress, how to comport myself as a lady," she waved a fork with a teasing smile, "how to eat in high society. I think she has been a success."

Alain nodded, his eyes glowing like emerald coals. "There is a mantle of sophistication about you now."

Cecile challenged his frankness. "Do you find it to your liking?" She reached for her wineglass, her gaze holding his over the rim of the crystal goblet.

"I would have liked you as much without it," Alain responded.

Cecile lowered her eyes at the compliment. "I'll always be that girl, Alain." She said quietly. "Etiquette and satins are nothing more than window dressing."

"Yes, and thank goodness for that. I will always love the girl I met in Paris who was poor but wouldn't take money to inform on her neighbors."

Alain reached for the decanter of wine to refill her goblet.

Cecile waved him off. "No, one glass is all I want."

"Very well," Alain replaced the decanter on the table. Silence stretched between them. Alain cleared his throat, his voice low and quiet when he spoke again. "Cecile, may I ask what happened that night in Le Havre?"

It was a difficult question, but Cecile knew there

would be one more question tonight that would be even more difficult to answer. "I was arrested in Le Havre." It would be easier to tell the tale without looking at Alain, but she knew she had to see every reaction on his face.

"To my credit, I led them a merry chase, as the English would say. I kept them hunting me long enough for you to get underway and to safety, which was my goal, my only goal. I couldn't bear the thought of everyone suffering when I could prevent it. Of all of us, I had the best chance of surviving such an arrest. I had men who admired me, for whatever reason, in high places. Even in the group of soldiers on the wharf, there was one who had courted me in hopes of favors."

Alain's emerald eyes flared. His hand played idly with the stem of his goblet. "I wouldn't have had you buy my freedom with your body." A grim edge tinted his voice.

"Then you'd have been a fool. A dead fool, and the rest of us dead with you." Cecile said bluntly. "Before I tell you what happened, let me tell you what I have learned since we parted. My family's motto was *la vérité ou rien* do you know it?

"The truth or nothing," Alain translated.

"I learned the night I lied for you at the general's that truth has its place but its place is not absolute, not when it means death for good people. My father never learned that and it got him an early grave. I learned I had power of my own if I would just seize it. Until Le Havre, I had lived my life as a victim. I didn't realize it at the time, but I'd spent the years since my parents' deaths believing I could not change the world. It didn't matter if Napoleon was in power or if a king sat on a throne. I realize now that I just had to change myself. I can't change the world, but I can mold myself to better face its challenges and in some small way, I might change the world a little. You helped me see that, and Le Havre proved it.

"Yes, I spent unpleasant months under house arrest at General Motrineau's, not knowing my sentence. I thought I was awaiting a trial, but in the end, word got to General Motrineau and I was freed without a trial or a sentence or any stigma on my name. I was free to go."

"Why did you not come to me?" Alain cried.

"Shh, Alain, mon cheri." Cecile shook her head, sensing the hurt he must feel. She had been alive and he'd been mourning her all the while. "Let me explain. I knew I had been pardoned without blemish in part because of the general's influence but also in part because there were people who still hoped to catch L'Un. They still believed I knew who he was and where he was. If I were free, I could lead them to him." She seized Alain's hands. "Mon cheri, if I had come to you, they would have hunted you down and I would have forfeited your life all for the vanity of my love. I had no money so I went to Nicholas Lupot and he took me on as an apprentice of sorts. It occupied my time and threw the circle of private citizens who wanted to see you dead off your trail." Cecile paused to let the import of her words settle as waiters entered with raspberry trifle syllabub with raspberry coulis and black currant almond tarte topped with almond liqueur.

When they left, Cecile took a bite of the fluffy dessert. "Now, tell me all about Etienne. Is my brother well?"

Talk of Etienne took the remainder of dessert and after

dinner drinks. Cecile's heart soared with Alain's news of Etienne's success and education. Her brother was thriving and happy. It was all she could wish for him.

When the last of the dishes had been removed, they rose and gathered their things. Alain swung his opera cloak proficiently around his shoulders, and then proceeded to drape Cecile's pelisse about her. His hands brushed the bare skin of her shoulder and she trembled at the intimate contact. A moment later, his lips pressed against the sensitive pulse at her neck, his hands still firm on her shoulders where the pelisse rested. She arched against him until her head rested on his shoulder. What heaven it was to give into such temptation.

Gallantly, Alain handed her into a hired carriage. They would be able to take the carriage together since she had been fortunate enough to have a townhouse on loan for the duration of her stay. The house was in a quiet, respectable part of Belgravia, just blocks from Alain's own lodgings.

They spoke only small talk as the carriage carried them across town. Alain pointed out sights of interest, offering to take her sightseeing soon to see the famous places up close. But underneath the quiet conversation, something more lively sparked and jumped between them. As the carriage drew to a halt, they risked one more kiss.

Alain jumped down and handed her out of the carriage, holding her about the waist longer than necessary. "I will call for you at eleven tomorrow. It's been a remarkable evening, spent with a remarkable woman."

Cecile bit her lip, uncertainly, hesitating for a moment. "Would you like to come in? Mrs. Brown will have retired."

Alain bent over her gloved hand and kissed it, palm side up. "Oh yes, dearest. I want to come in," he said in low, intimate tones. "But I am a gentleman and you are a lady of impeccable virtue. It would not be right."

Cecile nodded. "Until tomorrow then."

Alain drew her close. "Tonight, Cecile, we talked of the past. Tomorrow, we shall talk of the future, our future."

"I wish it were tomorrow already." She gave him a soft smile and fled into the house, completely aware of the message burning in his eyes.

Alain watched her until she disappeared inside the house. He paid the driver and dismissed him. He would walk the blocks to his lodgings. The energy coursing through him would not tolerate the confines of a carriage. His step was light and his heart jubilant as he set out. Cecile was alive! Cecile loved him! Plans reeled through his head in gleeful chaos. There would be letters to write. He'd need to post one immediately to Isabella and Tristan, who were rusticating in the country with their new son. There was a wedding to plan. He would marry her as quickly as it could be arranged. He didn't want a single second to go by without Cecile by his side. There was much he wanted to show her, to do with her, and much to amend for.

The only blot on his happy horizon was the knowledge that she had stayed away in order to protect him. He should have gone back no matter the risk to his safety, no matter the minimal odds of success. If he had gone, he might have found a way to rescue her and spirit her off to England years earlier.

Alain firmly pushed the damnable "what ifs" aside. He was going to claim happiness with both hands. His life had started again after a three year hiatus and he was anxious to live it. He laughed out loud to the night. He was getting married! At last, Fate had smiled on him.

Chapter Twelve

Alain discovered eleven o'clock was too long to wait in spite of London protocol that suggested strongly that a call could not be made earlier. He had risen early and ridden straight to Lambeth Palace to roust the archbishop for a special license, not caring that the man had just sat down to breakfast. By 10:30 he could wait no longer. He pulled the curricle he'd borrowed from Tristan's unused home in town up to Cecile's residence and bounded up the steps.

Mrs. Brown answered the door and gave him a strong perusal with her knowing her eyes. "Miss Cecile is waiting for you." The dour woman gave a small smile of approval.

Alain stepped into the foyer and laughed. Cecile was just as anxious as he. She stood in the doorway of the drawing room, making no pretense of having been waiting for him. She was already outfitted in her gloves and hat, ready to go the moment he arrived.

I could not wait." She gave a Gallic shru̱
ᴉoulders.

"Neither could I. At least I won't have to apo̱
for being early." Alain strode to her side and wa̱
kissed her cheek, aware that to dare more would e̱
Mrs. Brown's disapproval.

The day was warm, sprinkled with a spring breeze,
the perfect day for a drive through Hyde Park. They
drove leisurely, Cecile's arm tucked through his while
they tooled the paths, stopping every so often for introductions. Alain was proud to introduce the vibrant
beauty at his side to those they met, and Cecile was
pleasant and friendly to everyone as if she'd known
them for ages.

"What a perfect day!" Cecile exclaimed when they'd
left the last of the carriages behind on the verge.

"It could be like this always." Alain tempted, turning
the curricle towards Rutledge Pond. Alain smiled at
her, his green eyes confident and merry. "I've planned a
picnic for us." He parked the curricle beneath a spreading tree and jumped down to help Cecile. "I have all
your favorites. I believe you mentioned wine and
cheese last night." Alain teased, his hands at her waist
reveling at the feel of her slim form beneath the blue
muslin.

"And bread. I did mention bread too." Cecile teased
in return, crying out girlishly when Alain gave her a
playful twirl before setting her down.

Alain knew he should resist. They were in a public
place where anyone might spy them, but the spring day
and his own heady euphoria overrode his better judgment. Cecile looked far too beautiful in her blue gown

with its white lace, her bonnet falling back to reveal her chestnut hair, thick and lustrous in the sun. "I love you." He whispered for her alone before he bent to claim her lips in a deep kiss, uncaring of who might see this public declaration of affection for the woman who would be his wife.

Together they spread the picnic blanket on the grass and set out the food. Alain poured the wine. Cecile cut the crusty bread he'd bought fresh that morning. She popped a morsel into her mouth and chewed it speculatively. "Hmm. It's good enough for city fare." She offered. "I will make you real country bread."

Alain laughed at that. His mother, gracious lady that she was, would not have been caught baking bread for her baron. In fact, he doubted any of the Wickham baronesses baked bread. But his would. None of the barons had ever built a seaside resort either. He and Cecile would make their own trends. They were part of the new world he envisioned where class didn't bar anyone from opportunities. "I can hardly wait for your bread, but the Panchettes might feel you offer competition." Alain remarked, taking a thick slice from Cecile.

"The Panchettes! How are they? How good it will be to see them again."

"They are well and thriving." Alain proceeded to regale her with tales of French families in Hythe, of the Panchettes and their tea house, of the fabulous desserts their cousin made up at The Refuge for him nightly.

He leaned back on the blanket, hands behind his head, utterly content from the wine, the bread, and Cecile's laughter over his stories of Hythe. A man could be happy forever living on such simple pleasures. "I can hardly wait for you to be there with me, to see it at last." He was about to reach for her when a shrill voice broke their idyll.

"Dear Wickham, how good to see you!" She cooed from her seat in her carriage up on the pathway where she was surrounded by a coterie of matrons in similar vehicles, some of them accompanied by moonstruck young daughters who openly ogled him with embarrassing frankness.

He tossed Cecile a covert look of annoyance but once acknowledged, he had no choice except to rise and greet the woman. "Good day, Lady Halverston. Ladies." He offered a hand to Cecile and helped her rise. He led her to the verge, ready to make introductions, but Lady Halverston didn't let him get a word in before she started rambling. He expected the old biddy had suspicions about Cecile's presence and what it foretold. Her prattle was an attempt to waylay news she would find most unpleasant. Of all the things he'd looked forward to in regards to marriage with Alicia, his new mother-in-law was not one of them. The biddy would not cow him. He would meet her head on.

"It's not healthy for a young man like yourself to hide away in the country. We have been so worried about you. At least it looks like you've been taking care of yourself." She made an aside to the other ladies, "Wickham is always so well turned out, my Alicia appreciated that about him."

To Alain she said, "I was just telling the ladies how the new marble marker for Alicia's grave has arrived at last. You know how much time we spent finding the perfect sculptor and the right marble design. I know you'll appreciate the finished product. I hope you'll stop by the cemetery in Kent and see it. We sent all the way to Italy for the workmanship and the Carrera marble."

The woman affected some tears and groped dramatically for a handkerchief. "Oh my, I still get so overwrought about it. Just thinking about the tragedy still waters me up. If only you had been there that day, dear Wickham. I know you would have stopped the carriage in time." She waved her handkerchief. "Here I am acting like a watering pot in front of your friend. After such a display, Wickham, I am afraid you must introduce us."

"Lady Halverston, I would like to present Mademoiselle Cecile," Alain offered, unmoved by the display of tears. If anything, the display had prompted his disdain instead of his sympathy.

"The actress who's been performing at the Royal Opera House? How lovely for you to find someone to pass the time with, Wickham."

"The violinist," Cecile ground out with the barest civility. Alain gave her arm a gentle squeeze, counseling restraint. He was fully aware of what the woman implied and how she insulted Cecile with her comments. But it was not Cecile's place to respond. It was his, and he would.

"What was that? Violinist? Yes of course, if you prefer." The woman said airily, clearly suggesting she found the terms one and the same when it came to any woman performing in any manner at the opera house.

"Lady Halverston, I believe I failed to mention earlier that Cecile is my fiancée. We intend to marry in Hythe as soon as possible. I have a special license from the archbishop himself, issued just this morning." Alain was all smiles and charm as he delivered his news.

Lady Halverston spluttered the requisite good wishes and Alain let her recover her dignity as best she could. He nodded his farewell and turned Cecile back to the picnic blanket.

But the spring magic of the picnic was lost. Cecile was quiet, the earlier joy gone from her face. Alain knew she was hurting from the woman's comments.

"I am sorry. She is a difficult woman." Alain apologized at once.

"She's a mother without her child. Her grief must be very great," Cecile offered quietly, folding a cloth napkin around the remainder of the loaf.

"It's true she doted on Alicia. I fear she wishes to chain me to those memories as well. Every time we meet, there is always some indelicate reference to the tragedy our families shared," Alain said in equal quietness. "I was fond of Alicia, but it took meeting you for me to realize I didn't love her, not the way I imagined I would love a wife. It is you I want, you I can imagine being with."

"Alain, are you sure? Can these people accept that the Baron Wickham married a poor French girl of insignificant origins?"

Alain sensed the significance of her doubt. He

wanted to shake her and tell her the doubt was utter silliness, but he could see that it was all seriousness to her. He must handle this gently or risk losing her out of some sense of self sacrifice that prompted her to protect him.

"I can't believe the determined French girl I met in Paris would let such a minor thing as other people's opinions get in the way of what her heart wants. Your heart wants me. It is not arrogant to say it. It is true. You cannot tell me the passion in our kisses is that of an idle affair or that we could be happy apart. These people's opinions cannot be our undoing." He pressed.

"Have you considered that I love you too much to watch you suffer? There would be no joy in being your wife knowing that I brought you the scorn of your friends," Cecile said softly.

"Then love me a little less. I do not want another woman sacrificing herself for my benefit."

"What do you mean?" Cecile bristled and Alain wished he could retract the sharp words.

"Walk with me and I will tell you." There was a duck pond not far and they set out in that direction.

"My sister, Isabella, whom I have mentioned to you before, married a man—her first husband—in order to save the family title for me," Alain began as they walked. "She hardly knew him. He was in his fifties. She was nineteen. He was a rich marquess and he fancied her. My father was a good man but he had no head for business. He made some investments that overextended our funds, to put it simply. Isabella had a decent marriage with him but it was not the marriage she wanted." Alain explained. "I knew why she did it. It was for me, so that I'd have something other than debts and a meaningless title to inherit. I would have had to have found an heiress or an occupation if it hadn't been for her."

"Between your heroics and my sister's sacrifice, the two of you risk reducing me to feeling quite useless." Alain sighed. He bent over to pick up small pebbles and toss them into the duck pond.

Cecile rewarded him with a half smile. "That explains why you feel so responsible for everyone. I think you're trying to prove yourself without understanding you already have. Don't you see? It is because you're so worthy that people want to sacrifice for you. You shouldn't view it as a curse or a ghost to battle."

"Nonetheless, I love you Cecile, and I can't settle for the martyrdom of giving our love up simply because there might be hardships."

Cecile nodded. "That woman today was overwrought, but she spoke a truth we both must face. I'll never be one of them. Plenty of them will resent me for it."

Alain winked reassuringly. "But not me, Cecile. Not me." He sealed his promise with a kiss that spoke the depth of his devotion. Cecile was breathless when they parted.

"Is it true you have a special license?" Cecile asked, the twinkle returning to her sherry eyes.

"Let us leave for Hythe in the morning so I can prove it to you." Alain answered. "I cannot wait longer than I must to have you as my wife in all ways."

The journey to Hythe took a frustrating four days by carriage, stopping at inns and doing everything by the book to appease the watchful eye of Mrs. Brown, who took her role as secretary and chaperone to Cecile more seriously than Alain would have liked.

But as the village drew near on the fourth day, excitement mounted in him, mixed with anxiety.

Had anyone asked him, Alain would have classified himself as a confident man who was well aware of his charms and habits. Today his confidence was strangely lacking. What would Cecile think of the sleepy little town? True, it wasn't so sleepy anymore since the resort had been built. But it wasn't London or Paris, or even Brighton. Perhaps he had exaggerated Hythe's quality, built up her expectations too much. Would the Panchette's bakery and tea room appeal to her? It was a little place, nothing at all like Rules and the fine restaurants of London. Would The Refuge meet her expectations? It was a Tudor-style manor with decidedly male and rustic airs about it.

He'd once been certain the young girl he'd courted in Paris would have loved Hythe. But the sophisticated, self-made woman who traveled around Europe entertaining in the homes of the elite might find his home lacking, his town boring. What could possibly appeal to her about the middle-class resort he'd established?

They approached the hill overlooking the seaside town, and Alain had the carriage pull off the road. "We're nearly there, Cecile. Come and see Hythe from the cliff. It's my favorite vantage point." He handed her down from the carriage, pride and nerves mingling unpleasantly in his belly.

Cecile smiled at him softly, and he wondered if she

divined the source of his apprehension. "I will love it because it is yours, Alain." She assured him.

At the cliff edge she gasped in delight. "Oh Alain, it is all you told me and more. She pointed with a hand. "Is that the hotel? The one where Etienne works?"

"Yes." Alain beamed, proud that she'd spotted the building he'd so diligently poured his heart into. He stood behind her, an arm about her waist, and directed her gaze with his free arm. "There's the Panchette's tea house, two buildings down from the hotel on the right."

Cecile sighed and leaned against him. "It is as I dreamed it would be."

Alain felt the tension seep from him and they stood there in silence, letting the blue sky and the spring weather work their magic. Hythe gleamed jewel-like below them and the Channel sparkled beyond the rim of the town. The feeling of homecoming coursed through his veins. With his resort a success and Cecile in his arms, he was complete—not again but perhaps for the first time ever.

Behind them, Mrs. Brown coughed discreetly to indicate the need to move on. Cecile turned in the arc of Alain's arms, smiling up at him and twining her hands about his neck. "We've seen your town, now take me to your home, mon cheri."

The Refuge was not far and they were there within minutes, Cecile's head poking out of the carriage in her eagerness to see it. Alain laughed at her obvious impatience but did nothing to pull her back inside, letting her enjoy the excitement. He loved that everything was fresh and new when seen through Cecile's sherry eyes.

The carriage turned onto the parkland drive leading to The Refuge and the anticipation of being at journey's end seized him as well. The rambling Tudor-styled structure came into view. Cecile popped her head back into the carriage, her eyes wide.

"Alain, it's huge! From your descriptions, I imagined it was a hunting lodge, maybe a five-room cottage, which would have been big enough for me." She was nearly breathless with her discovery.

"It is small compared to the estate in the Lake District." Alain said easily. Their conveyance rocked to a halt in the half-circle drive and Alain let her take in the Tudor estate for several moments before ushering her indoors.

Inside, Harker had the modest staff waiting in a neat line to greet them but Cecile was more entranced with the entry. So enrapt with the hall, she hardly noticed them. She turned around in a slow, complete circle in the entry, gazing at the medieval-styled wooden rafters and the long wall hung with an authentic tapestry that added to the older feel of the hall. A simple, high narrow table of dark wood was positioned beneath the tapestry just as it might have been in a lord's grand hall centuries ago.

"My lord, welcome home." Harker came forward, clearing his throat to get Cecile's attention.

Alain watched her. Would she blush at her indiscretion or would she carry off the behavior with aplomb.

Cecile stopped her investigation of the foyer and straightened, taking in the discreet staff, seeing them for perhaps the first time, Alain realized. "The hall is overwhelming." She said without apology. "You must be Harker. Alain has told me all about you, how you run this place with precision."

Harker preened under the compliment, and Alain smiled at Cecile's way with people. She would do well here. His people would respond to her brand of leadership. She'd deal with them the same way she'd dealt with the people in her neighborhood in Paris—with skill and sensitivity. She was born to be the compassionate lady of the manor, his manor. He was all but forgotten as Harker introduced her to the small staff.

As Cecile conversed with the pastry chef, Harker signaled for Alain's attention. "She's wonderful, isn't she, Harker?" Alain said, thinking his opinionated butler wanted to offer his stamp of approval on Cecile.

"Oh, no doubt, my lord. She's splendid, just like your mother was and French too. Who would have thought The Refuge would see two French mistresses." Harker offered, then rushed on after his sentimental indulgence. "What I wanted to tell you, was that Daniel is waiting for you in the library. He said it was urgent. He's ridden hard to get here."

It was not like Daniel to express false urgency. Worry pitted Alain's stomach. He gently interrupted Cecile's conversation and clasped Cecile's hand in apology. "I am afraid the tour will have to wait. I need to go up and see what news my friend has brought. Harker can show you to your room. I'll be with you shortly." This wasn't the homecoming he'd planned. He'd wanted to give Cecile a quiet, leisurely tour of his home without any intrusions, stroll the woodlands with her.

"Daniel, I'm home," Alain said, stepping into the

book-lined room. "Harker said it was of the highest priority."

Daniel wore a stern look on his face. "It is most urgent." His eyes glanced about the room. "You are alone?"

"Currently. Harker is showing Cecile to her room."

"Good. I am not too late then. I've come to warn you that you've brought home a traitor."

Alain furrowed his brow. He did not comprehend Daniel's message in the least. He folded himself into a chair. "Mrs. Brown? The chaperone is a traitor? I admit I don't know a thing about her only that she's Cecile's secretary," he rambled, searching for comprehension.

"No, Alain. Not Mrs. Brown, whoever she is." Daniel leaned forward patiently, hands splayed on tan breeches, his voice gentle as he delivered his news. "Cecile. The traitor is Cecile."

"Cecile? A traitor of what? Whatever are you talking about?" Alain was too deep in confusion to be shocked yet by Daniel's statement.

"I am talking about the person who betrayed L'Un at the docks, the person who betrayed secretary Ramboulet." Daniel said succinctly.

Alain was all stiff defiance. "That claim is impossible and patently false. She is to be my wife."

"Please, Alain, listen to what I have to say. I would not come here to wreck your happiness without just cause," Daniel pleaded cautiously.

Alain leaned back in his chair and exhaled heavily. "Alright, tell me what you know."

Slowly, Daniel held forth a crumpled piece of paper, worn and tattered about the edges. "It seems the game you played in Paris was deeper than I understood with spies and counterspies and secret societies abounding from every corner," he said, his voice tinged with sadness at having been left out of his friend's thoughts, his friend's agony.

Alain felt guilty. Daniel had stood him well in his friendship and yet he had not once included Daniel in the changes that had occurred in his life, or the grief that had encompassed the last three years. But it wasn't only Daniel he'd left out, he had told no one of the burden his heart carried. Perhaps he should have.

Alain reached out and took the paper. He smoothed it on his knee and read. It was in French of course. He read it once then twice to make sure he had the translation correct. He did. The document was a confession of patriotism to the now defunct government of Napoleon with Cecile's name signed neatly, legibly, at the bottom, owning to traveling in L'Un's company for the express purpose of compromising Pierre Ramboulet and unmasking L'Un.

It was so at odds to everything Cecile had explained over dinner but the magic of that wondrous night seemed far away now in light of this development. "Where did you get this?"

"You know how Tristan and Isabella worry over you," Daniel shrugged. "Tristan knows everyone at Whitehall from his experience in the wars, and I think he and Isabella sensed your grief over the death of the accomplice. When there was no more news forthcoming about the person, it seems Tristan took it upon himself to look into it. An associate of his in the Foreign Office stumbled across this during a diplomatic mission in Paris a month or so ago."

Later, when the anger and hurt faded, Alain divined he'd been touched by his friend's efforts. Although he was close to Daniel, Tristan was a friend from his boyhood, the most trusted friend he'd ever known. When others had not fathomed the depth of his feelings over the unknown accomplice's death, Tristan had intuitively recognized its import to him. Tristan had acted even though Alain had chosen to shut him and others out of his private mourning. Tristan had asked only once about the violin over the hearth and then had the good sense to say no more. But it had been enough to put him on the scent.

Alain glanced back at the paper and bits of the conversation over dinner at Rules began to take on new perspectives. She had been under house arrest, not sent to a dank prison like so many others. She'd had friends in influential places. All she'd had to do was sign her name to a piece of paper and she was saved.

For a moment his heart leapt. What was that she'd said about her redefining of her family motto? Ah yes—that she understood now there were circumstances when a lie served better. His mind's logic crushed the surge of hope. If there was a lie interwoven amongst the truths, what was it? It could be the piece of paper—a signature for her freedom, a very small price to pay to ward off the certainty of death. It could just as easily be the lie behind why she did not come to him for three years. She had not come out of fear of betraying him to assassins as she'd said.

Oh God, this was getting murkier by the moment. Why had she come now? Dark scenarios clamored for his attention. Alain put his head in his hands in an effort to stifle the irrational thoughts. He clung to the instinctive answer he knew to be true in his heart. Cecile was not a traitor. She had not betrayed him. She was neither a traitor to L'Un as indicated by the paper he held, nor the accomplice gossiped about years earlier.

"What are you going to do?" Daniel asked quietly.

Alain lifted his head. He'd entirely forgotten Daniel was still there. "I must tell Cecile. I must ask her about this paper."

"She may not admit to it. She has no reason to incriminate herself." Daniel shook his head, wary of Alain's idea.

"Still, I cannot resolve this situation making half-guesses on my own." Alain rose and went to the door.

"Alain, I am sorry to bring you the news. Tristan offered to come but he feared he would be too late."

"It's alright." Alain felt his friend's need for absolution. "It was right to tell me even though it is news I'd rather not know. I am glad for it. How much harder it would be to find this out later, once I was married."

Harker was in the hall waiting for him when he exited the study. "I have put Miss Cecile in the room overlooking the gardens, my lord. A maid is with her helping with the unpacking."

The man was clearly anxious over Daniel's news but Alain kept it to himself. He pasted on a smile. "Very good, Harker. I'll go up and see how she is settling in."

Alain strode up the staircase, his heart pounding with every step that brought him closer to Cecile's room. Once he went through that door, he'd have to face the answers to the questions that troubled him most: why had Cecile signed the paper? Had she lied to him in London? If so, why had she come to him now? Alain gripped the door knob hard with his right hand, taking a moment to rest his head against the door frame and gather his strength. He had never run from unpleasant encounters in his life. He wasn't going to start now—not with his future at stake.

Chapter Thirteen

"Alain! This room is wonderful." Cecile exclaimed when he entered the room. "I've opened the windows to let in the sun and the beautiful day." Her face glowed, open and happy. She looked perfectly placed surrounded as she was by white furniture and the rose papered walls, her trunks open, clothing strewn on the bed. If he'd been an artist he would have painted this scene and captured the moment forever—a young woman so clearly in love, unpacking for the first time in her fiancé's home.

His heart lurched at the duty he came to do. It seemed an obvious disservice to bring up such sordid things.

Cecile tugged playfully on his hand. "Come to the window. You can smell the lilac bushes. It's like nature's own sachet."

Alain went to the window with her and breathed deeply the smells of The Refuge in spring. It was a smell

172

he loved—lilacs mixed with honeysuckle and the faint overlay of the roses that grew further out in the gardens. Cecile breathed it in too, closing her eyes and giving herself over to the delights of nature in full bloom. Watching her drink it in, he wanted to throw away Daniel's crumpled paper, wanted to forget such a thing existed. But his heart and mind prompted action with their silent counsel: *"Ask her. She loves you, you saw the depth of her love moments ago when you looked in her face and saw her abject happiness over the room, you saw it just now as she breathed in the scent of the land you love. She will forgive you if you're wrong. She loves you. She has never been anything but goodness itself . . . She loves you . . . she loves you. . . ."*

"It is no wonder you love this place, Alain." Cecile said, opening her eyes. "I love it too. I never stopped being a country girl at heart even after years in Paris. Might we go down and stroll in the garden? I could pick some flowers for dinner. Harker mentioned Etienne would be coming up. I can hardly wait to see him." She stopped suddenly in her excited chatter. "What is it, Alain? Was there bad news waiting for you?" Cecile reached up a hand to smooth away the furrow on his brow. Her touch was soft and cool.

Alain took her hand and kissed it. "Let's go walk in the garden. I find I have something to ask you."

The quiet warmth of the garden surrounded them. It was still enough in the garden to hear the bees at work in the flowers. Further in, Cecile caught the burble of a fountain hidden by a screen of square hedges. She would love caring for this garden. It had been ages since she'd had a garden to tend and never anything as extensive as this. She bent over a lilac bush and inhaled. Something was bothering Alain, but she would patiently wait until he wanted to share.

They strolled around the next corner into a pretty alcove decorated with a low stone bench surrounded by climbing roses. Alain gestured for her to sit. She looked at him expectantly. He did not sit. He paced the ground in front of her. She tried cajolery. "Alain, whatever it is, we'll resolve it together. It can't be as bad as all this." His anxiety was contagious. If he was worried, perhaps she should be worried too. But what was there to worry about?

"Is it Etienne?" she asked cautiously, unable to think of large concern that encompassed them both.

Alain stopped pacing. "No. I am sorry, Cecile. What I have to say is sordid and low but I find it must be said if we're to have any hope of a future." Alain reached into his pocket and pulled out a piece of paper. "Daniel brought this with him. It's a paper, signed by you, confessing to the betrayal of Pierre Ramboulet which led to his execution."

Cecile clamped a hand to her mouth. The paper that she'd signed because it hadn't mattered. It had been a harmless act at the time, but now she saw it from Alain's perspective, saw the fear of damnation, and the belief that she'd lied to him in his sharp green eyes. Her claim on happiness was suddenly quite tenuous indeed. "Oh Alain, you don't believe it do you?" She gasped in her hurt.

"I don't want to believe it but I am not sure it can be so easily discarded. Is this not your signature? Did someone sign your name without your knowledge? Were you coerced to bear false testimony?"

Cecile knew Alain was grasping at straws, rational excuses he'd concocted to justify the existence of her name on the paper. She could seize one of them and allay his suspicions for good and claim her happiness. She could tell him the general had forced her to sign it, which wasn't all false, just not the harrowing coercion Alain would conjure up in his mind. But it was the truth or nothing. She would not, could not build their future on a foundation of half-truths.

Cecile met his gaze evenly, her hands clenched tightly in the lap of her gown. "It is my signature, Alain. No one forced me to do it. I chose to sign the paper."

Alain stifled a moan and sank to the low bench. "Oh God. How? Why? I loved you, I trusted you with my life and you gave Motrineau the final validation he needed to arrest Ramboulet."

It was Cecile's turn to stand and pace. She was utterly undone by Alain's distress and the depths of the betrayal he thought her capable of. "Let me explain, Alain. It's not exactly how you think. I did not betray you." Desperation threatened to swamp her. She had not fought for three years to have it end this way—with him believing she had lied to him. She felt very much like the little boy who held the dike by plugging it with his finger. Except she'd be plugging the hole with words, words that had to be meticulously chosen in her fledgling English.

"Motrineau was willing to help me clear my name in exchange for a favor. He needed to make his household look heroic, in case the French managed to be victorious in battle. He didn't want Napoleon questioning his loyalties. It looked suspicious that the secretary had been a traitor and that Motrineau had done nothing about him for so long. Enter me. Motrineau said he'd see to my release if I signed a paper stating I had turned in the secretary. This way, his household looked as if it had been plotting to catch the poor man all along and it explained why I had been in Le Havre." She held her breath, letting Alain ingest the information. Alain's head lifted, studying her.

She went on. "Of course, my signature looked suspicious since I'd been caught with L'Un at the Le Havre docks. My presence with L'Un made Motrineau look like a traitor who had been supporting Napoleon's enemies the whole while. We had to explain my presence with L'Un in order to make everything look legitimate.

"By 'turning in' the secretary, I could pretend that Ramboulet told us the identity of L'Un, that I infiltrated L'Un's ranks in order to lead Motrineau's men to him." Cecile sighed. "I didn't think it mattered except to protect you and yes, to protect myself. The secretary was already dead. Signing the paper couldn't hurt him any more. Signing the paper couldn't hurt you, couldn't expose you any further. But it could save us, buy us time. Then Napoleon was defeated and I figured the paper had been lost. The confession was useless. It was certainly a useless piece of paper since no one would be checking out the loyalties of a regular citizen at that point."

Cecile fell to her knees before him and clasped his long hands tightly. "I did not think the paper would resurface in such a disastrous way. Your friend told you what he knew, thinking it best for you. But he did not know everything. I have never lied to you."

Her unspoken message hung between them. He had lied to her about his identity. *He* had created a complete fabrication and yet she had forgiven him enough to risk her life for his. She had forgiven him for much more than she was asking him for. She wasn't even asking for forgiveness. She was simply asking to be believed.

Alain let his mind empty of all logic and thought except the cool grip of Cecile's hands on his. If he didn't believe her now on her own merits, they would never have trust between them. He could not ask Tristan to check her story. He had to decide this on his own and he had to decide it right now. To sleep on it would only cast doubt on whether or not it was she he completely believed or if he'd had time to collaborate her story with outside information. Everything between them had come down to this moment, this decision.

Cecile understood it too. Alain could hear only the faintest of breaths as she sat motionless waiting for his pronouncement. In the silence, he remembered a small bit of wisdom from his father when he was growing up: the things regretted in life are the things not done. Alain knew he regretted plenty of things he'd elected not to do, like riding out to meet the carriage that fateful day. He did not regret the chance he'd taken to build the resort, or to rescue the Panchettes from France. He would not live the rest of his life regretting his choice to let Cecile go because he was too frightened to grasp happiness with both hands.

He spoke the words that could bridge their rift,

knowing even as he spoke them, they might not be enough. "I believe you. You've been nothing but goodness since the day we met. I should not have doubted."

Cecile smiled. "Thank you, Alain."

Alain shook his head in denial. "I should not have brought it up. I should have told Daniel he misunderstood the information and dismissed it out of hand."

"Absolutely not. We must sort through these things together." A teasing sparkle lit her eyes and the joy she'd emanated earlier returned. "Now, what shall we do, Alain?"

"I believe the next order of business is the marriage proposal I made to you in London. Will you accept in spite of me making a muck of things? Please, Cecile, marry me. No other person in this world has risked as much for me as you have. You've risked your life and your heart. I can't pretend to be worthy of that, but I will spend my whole life working to earn it."

Joy suffused her face in a rapturous glow. "I find I can't turn the offer down." She leaned forward and kissed him with all the love in her heart.

Chapter Fourteen

Cecile's wedding day dawned with a blue sky and fluffy white clouds. The Refuge was bursting with friends who'd arrived two days earlier for the festivities. Alain's sister, Isabella, had come with the new baby and her handsome husband, Tristan. Alain's two childhood friends, Giles and Chatham had come as well, eagerly agreeing to share a room with Daniel to make space for everyone at The Refuge.

Cecile and Etienne had been warmly embraced by Alain's friends and by the town. This morning Cecile had been awakened with breakfast in bed delivered by Isabella, who insisted she not worry about going downstairs until it was time to depart for St. Leonard's. Isabella had stayed with her, chatting and laughing while she bathed and the maid Alain had hired for her did up her hair and threaded it with pearls.

Cecile turned her head in the mirror, straining to see the elegant coiffure from all angles. "It's so lovely!"

179

she exclaimed. "But it seems a waste since I'll have a veil over it."

Isabella laughed. "Alain will be able to see it and that's all that matters. Come, it's time for the gown. People will want to stop by your room and say good-bye before they head for the church. We can't have them find you in dishabille."

Cecile stood patiently as the gown of silk glace was lifted over her head and gliding over the curves of her body. Isabella herself did up the pearl buttons at the back, exclaiming over the gown. It was of purest white, highwaisted and banded beneath her breasts with a pink satin ribbon. Because it was June, Cecile had foregone the long tight sleeves, opting instead for short puffed sleeves trimmed in graceful falls of delicate Honiton lace that matched the vandyked hem on the gown. The veil too was made of yards of Honiton lace.

"You look lovely. I'll only be the first one to tell you that today." Isabella said as they surveyed the gown in the mirror together. There was a knock on the door, and the procession of well wishers began, each of them exclaiming over Cecile's gown.

Finally the house grew quiet, the guests having departed for the church. Etienne was the last one to come to the room. It was Isabella's cue to depart for the church with her husband and baby. Etienne would give Cecile away.

"Are you ready, CeeCee?" Etienne asked. "I am to tell you that Alain has left for church with Tristan, so it's safe to come downstairs without him seeing you."

They laughed at the superstition, both a little nervous over what the day would hold for them.

"We've come a long way," Cecile said.

Etienne nodded. "You're a famous violin player and a baroness now. Who would have thought?"

"You're still my brother. Nothing has changed that. The Refuge will be your home too."

"I know. I like Alain. He has been a good mentor for me. We have talked about my future. He has arranged for me to go to London and study the hotel industry at one of the best hotels in town so that I have my options. Ideally he wants me to come back and take over the resort, but I am not sure yet."

Cecile nodded. "You will be good at it."

"And you will be good for him. I can see it in the way he looks at you." Etienne clasped his sister's hand. "Time to go."

The journey from The Refuge to St. Leonard's was a happy one. Cecile rode in an open landau decorated with flowers and satin ribbons. The streets were lined with the citizens of Hythe who had turned out to greet the baron's new wife. They threw flowers while she laughed and caught at them.

But nothing compared to the joy she felt when the doors to St. Leonard's opened, revealing Alain standing in full morning dress at the end of a flower bedecked aisle. The church was turned out in its best, with flowers along the side aisles as well, and the pews packed with Alain's friends dressed in their summer finest for the occasion.

Music came from a hidden place, a string quartet she guessed. How thoughtful of Alain to provide music from the instrument she so dearly loved. Etienne walked her down the long aisle to where her new husband waited. Tristan stood next to him, and Mrs. Brown waited as her own witness. Cecile recognized some of the faces as she passed. Isabella gave her a teary smile while she juggled the baby. Then she was next to Alain and all else faded.

They had waited three years for this. Alain covered her hand with his own, warm and strong, lending his support should she need it.

The vicar began. Cecile supposed the service was nice and words meaningful but nothing could dislodge her attention from the emerald-eyed, golden-haired jewel of a man who stood beside her pledging his fidelity and love and the future they would make together. At last the ceremony was complete. The vicar intoned the most romantic words of the ritual. "Baron Wickham, you may kiss the bride."

Alain bent to her and whispered, "Cecile, you're my hero. You have saved me in ways you cannot guess."

Cecile smiled. "No, you're mine. You're my heroic baron."

With that, they sealed their union with a kiss and turned to face their friends and their future together.